Cunval's Mission

CUNVAL'S MISSION

dinas

David Hancocks

© David Hancocks & Y Lolfa Cyf., 2004
First impression: 2004

This contents of this book are subject to copyright and may not be reproduced by any means without the prior written consent of the publishers.

Cover artwork:

ISBN: 0 86243 709 1

Dinas is an imprint of Y Lolfa

Printed and published in Wales
by Y Lolfa Cyf., Talybont, Ceredigion SY24 5AP
e-mail ylolfa@ylolfa.com
website www.ylolfa.com
tel. (01970) 832 304
fax 832 782

chapter 1

Cunval was a frightened young man. Although he was now twenty-one years of age, he had never been alone in his life. The Deacon, Aidan, had distressed him at the outset of his journey, by slyly joking that he would probably have his little body dissected by his new master, the fearsome Yarl Brockvael. Cunval well knew that his one over-riding weakness was a lack of confidence. How could he be the man for this important mission? His long years of tuition at Caerleon had not really prepared him for such a personal upheaval.

The journey, with a large backpack, was in itself meant to be an ordeal, an initiation into the difficulties that lay ahead. He was thankful that he was to visit two priests on the way; two former pupils at the Caerleon College: Brother Madoc, who had been the priest at Caer Bigga for three years, and Brother Tidiog, who had been successful in setting up a Christian community at far-off Abermenei. Cunval had heard the harrowing accounts of the abuse they had suffered in the early stages of their rural missions. This had depressed him; however, he had now been entrusted with his own pioneer parish, and he was not going to let his dear brothers down without a fight.

"Don't try to convert them all at once; lead by good example," was Bishop Dyfrig's instruction. Madoc, a fellow native of Ely, Cunval's home territory, west of Caer Taf, had a wicked sense of humour. His frivolous advice as Cunval was about to set off into the morning mist was, "If Brockvael is about to cut out your tongue, tell him that your mother is sleeping with the King."

Refreshed by a good night's rest and with some extra food from Madoc, Cunval set off to follow a small river eastwards. After a few hours, his feet were sore and his sandals chafed through his woollen socks. Now was the time to apply some of his practical knowledge; he rested by a spring and replenished his water bottle before taking a small iron axe from his pack. A broken alder tree provided him with the wood to fashion a rough pair of clogs, and these he tied to his feet with leather thongs. Stuffing his socks with damp moss in all the appropriate places, he strode up and down until satisfied that his potential blisters would be partially spared further distress. His stout staff was a great help.

Mid-March was Cunval's favourite time of the year. The songbirds had awakened, the trees were preparing for bud-burst, and the days were getting longer. In sheltered places on the ground, primroses and violets smiled up at him, and when the sun's rays reached through to him, they were warm and reassuring. He plodded on until mid-day, resting now and then and adjusting his footwear, all the while singing to keep up his spirits.

Cunval's pack was getting heavier and he needed to shed it for a while and rest his aching muscles. He had been following a track-way up through a small valley, and now came to a dry, sunny spot on the bank of stream. Thankfully unbuckling the straps of his backpack, he let it slide to the ground. After setting out his food on a cloth, he lay back on the grass, his head resting on his folded, hooded cape, his feet covered with his sheepskin square. He hummed contentedly whilst chewing on a crust.

Cunval must have dozed off to sleep. He awoke to feel a presence; there was no sound, just apprehension. Then, he was aware of a shadow and someone gripping his shoulders from behind. He shouted out in fear but could not move. Someone else was lying across his feet.

"Now, don't struggle, young priest, we're not going to hurt you."

The gruff, menacing voice told Cunval that he should do as requested. His heart was racing and, gripped with fear, he was terrified at the thought of a flashing knife.

"I won't run." spluttered Cunval. "Let me up." He could see neither assailant, but could smell an unwashed, rancid body.

"Easy now."

Cunval was pulled up to a sitting position. The teenage boy who had been gripping his feet now sat astride him, wild-eyed. An older, thickset man with a dirty beard and a leather cap knelt to one side of Cunval, a knife held loosely in his scabby hand. The look on Cunval's face and his fast-blinking wide eyes brought a contemptuous dismissal from the ruffian as he set about wolfing down Cunval's food. He motioned to the boy to join him.

"Thanks, Mocan," said the boy dutifully. He was also dirty.

"Is this clean water?" Mocan picked up Cunval's water bottle.

"Yes, of course," bleated Cunval. "I'm glad to share my

food with you."

"Share? Share?" Mocan laughed loudly. "Now, let's have a look in here." He wrenched at Cunval's backpack and pulled out the contents: leather pouches of seeds, medicines, carpenter's tools. All spilled out onto the grass.

"Please," begged Cunval. "These are all I have in the world. They're for my new home at Penhal."

"Penhal?" Mocan looked startled.

"Yes, I'm going to Yarl Brockvael's estate. He'll kill me if I turn up empty-handed. He doesn't like priests at the best of times."

Cunval, despite his terror, saw a brisk change in Mocan's countenance. Did he know of Brockvael?

"Bah! There's nothing here, boy," shouted Mocan. "Let's be off."

With that, the two robbers jumped the brook, scrambled up the bank and were soon out of sight. Cunval quickly packed his belongings and staggered off up the track-way, clutching his precious backpack. After a mile of puffing and wheezing, he scolded himself for not offering thanks to his Saviour. It was time to kneel and pray.

The rest of the afternoon he spent crossing moor land, travelling east and looking for his next landmark, the winding dark stream called the Trothee. Nervously, Cunval looked about the landscape. He saw smoke from the occasional farmstead, but dared not approach, for his confidence was shattered by the earlier harsh experience, and he did not want to be caught out by the approaching dusk. Soon he had followed the Trothee to a river that he had never seen before: the mighty Gwei. This was the old tribal boundary of the Cornovi, the most Romanised of the Celtic people and close allies of his own Silurian tribe. The Romans had left Britain almost a hundred years before, and, apart from the sparse scattering of Christianity, and the survival of the Roman tongue among the upper classes, the tribes had reverted to their old pagan ways. Rule was by the Kings and their families.

A footbridge gave Cunval a good view of the hills to the east and provided a final resting place before his last push upstream.

Walking through the outskirts of Abermenei, he aroused little interest among the adults, despite the significance of his brown woollen robe, his ear-to-ear shaven tonsure and his staff. Brother Tidiog had long been accepted as part of the town community, and this ready acceptance was encouraging. A group of children, however, started to throw stones at Cunval and called him a thumb-sucker; they knew that he could not retaliate.

"You can't throw very straight, can you?" jibed Cunval, ducking and weaving. He knew just how to handle children. The rough town kids of Caerleon had given him experience of juvenile human nature. He ran over to an elderly lady, took her arm affectionately and helped her with her firewood bundle.

"Aren't these children sweet?" he declared loudly. "I am certain that they would have offered to help you home."

The eldest boy, aged about ten, glared at Cunval, knowing that he had been outwitted. Cunval glared back as the old lady waved her stick at the boy.

"That's my grandson. He never does anything to help me."

The boy backed off and Cunval walked briskly over to

some men who were working a furnace.

"Good evening. Good evening." He smiled cheerfully. "I'm visiting Tidiog. Where does he live?" The men nodded up the road and carried on with their work.

The children caught up with Cunval again as he was leaving the town through the partly derelict, up-river gateway. However, somebody shouted at them and they left Cunval unmolested.

Tidiog was overwhelmed when Cunval, singing loudly, approached his enclosure.

"I never thought I would see a fellow priest again," roared Tidiog. "It's been so long. Aren't you young Cunval? When were you ordained? You were three years younger than me, when we were at college."

They clasped each other in a brotherly embrace and, laughing together, skipped towards Tidiog's humble hut. Tidiog was stocky and dark compared to Cunval, who had a short, gangling frame and wispy light hair.

"I have some wine. It's not very good; and, look, I was just making supper."

Cunval was very flattered and his spirits were lifted. He well remembered Tidiog at Caerleon – always a hard worker and popular with everybody.

"Now, tell me all the news. Is Bishop Dyfrig well? Is Aidan as crusty as ever? Who else has been given a parish?"

Tidiog's questions were endless, and Cunval loved the occasion. Even the story of his encounter with the robbers now seemed amusing. They talked and talked as the night closed in. The vegetable stew was tasty and the bread was fresh. Tidiog had carefully bathed Cunval's feet and rubbed them with a pungent ointment.

"More wine? What about some pork rib? Look, it's nice and fat and…"

"Yuk!" cried Cunval. "I just can't eat meat, and I'll take no more wine, thank you. I'm beginning to feel dizzy. Tell me again about your congregation."

"Well, as I say, sometimes as many as twelve people come here on a Sunday. I wish we could sing in their language instead of Latin; I'm sure that they would enjoy it more. Anyway, they are the same people whom I work with in the town, repairing the houses, farming, and looking after the gardens. That's how I do quite well for food, and acquire a little wine or cider. I've now done eight burials in my enclosure, and I get along very well with Pedur, the governor of Abermenei."

Cunval was staring blankly into the fire.

"I'm sorry, Cunval. I've been doing most of the talking. Look, I know exactly how you feel right now. You're a little apprehensive."

"Apprehensive! I'm terrified. If Brockvael throws me out, or worse, I'll just die. I'll have to go off into the forest and excommunicate myself for ever."

"No, no. Everything will work out, you'll see. Brockvael is an old man now; he dare not upset the King's bishop." Tidiog smiled reassuringly and patted Cunval on the shoulder.

They said their final prayers at Tidiog's small altar in the corner of the hut.

That night, Cunval slept fitfully. Wine always gave him vivid dreams, and he continually woke up in a sweat. Daylight was a relief. He went to the riverbank and said his prayers.

"How do you like my cemetery, Cunval? See, it's almost circular around the hut. I've been collecting stones from the river to mark the boundary. Soon, I'll have a proper wall. You see how I picked my spot on this raised ground?"

Cunval walked around, counting the graves with their small wooden crosses. Then, he paced out the boundary and measured the hut. He stood and admired the high wooden cross near the entrance.

"Mine will be just like this," enthused Cunval. "If I ever get the chance to have one!" They both laughed.

Tidiog put his arm round Cunval's shoulder. "Now, don't forget, come and see me in the summer, when you're settled."

After herb broth and bread, Cunval set off for the town. He was obliged to call on the King's trusted overseer, Pedur, an honourable, elderly man who had once been a battle leader for both King Emrys and King Myric. Pedur occupied the old Roman bathhouse, or what was left of it; he said that he wasn't interested in the new Christian nonsense; however, he did offer sympathy to any priest who was going to live at Penhal. The old Roman town was a shambles, a heap of rubble and ashes, with dogs barking and locked-up pigs squealing. The Celtic peasants had long forgotten Roman discipline. Food production was their only concern, and all the young men had been forced to join the King's army. The Saxons, far to the east, were a constant threat, and district administrators such as Pedur were obliged to keep law and order, but mainly in order to provide food and trained young men for the army.

Pedur's wife, a delightful lady called Elise, gave Cunval some oatcakes and a small jar of honey. Cunval thanked her kindly. As he left the bathhouse, a gang of children were playing in the street nearby. He called them over.

"I'm glad I saw you," he said, and smiled. "Can anyone tell me the way to Penhal?"

"I know," shouted a bright little girl. "You go to the river and then turn right." They all pointed helpfully.

"It will take you all day," scowled an older boy.

Cunval nodded. "Well, I hope to see you all later in the summer."

In good spirits, Cunval left the west gate and followed the pathway indicated. The fields between the town and the rivers were in the process of being ploughed; several of the labourers waved to him politely and this lifted his spirits. The children had started to follow, but Cunval's pace soon lost them. He had work to do and psalms to sing. The morning sun was warm as he approached his final river. When he finally turned north into the valley of the Menei, he knew that he was home. Although he had never set foot in the valley before, he knew that this was his destiny; the one place on earth that his bishop had had good reason to send him. The river water from the far mountains was crystal clear, with a succession of pools and rapids overhung with willow, alder and hazel. Cunval was adept at making fish traps; his favourite food was fish, fresh or smoked. He could not eat meat; it made him sick. However, he was well versed in animal husbandry, which had formed part of his monastic life, and gardening and farming were second nature to him.

He now relished each step of the way. After a mile or so, he realised that the riverbank was littered with piles of driftwood thrown up by the winter floods. This would mean a plentiful supply of dry firewood for the next winter. If

Yarl Brockvael granted him some land, he could plant his seeds and his wheat in April. There was going to be so much to do, if he was allowed time from his community chores.

Cunval reflected on his now-complete break with Caerleon. He had always been smaller than his contemporaries, but had made up for his lesser strength by being always keen and willing. He would run rather than walk, when sent on errands, and his enthusiasm when reading and citing the scriptures had always impressed his masters. As he had progressed through the college, he had been given the task of teaching the new, younger pupils. He knew well the nickname that they had given him: "Running Piglet". He laughed at the memories.

There was only one thing to do to allay his homesickness: he sang loudly, and he didn't care if anyone could hear him and think him mad. The day was long and arduous and Cunval had to stop many times to rest his feet.

chapter 2

Late in the afternoon, when Cunval realised he had about two hours of daylight left, he quickened his pace. It was starting to get cooler and he hoped that there would be food at Penhal. Travellers were almost always welcomed at estate halls. It was traditional to offer hospitality after a long journey and, after all, Cunval was expected. It had been a request of King Myric that all estates should have a trained priest, a learned man who was expected to toil in the fields and teach the community the Gospels, farming and good Christian values.

However, the king had not dared to interfere too much with the pagan gods of the country dwellers; they were often the very people who had fought with him against the Saxon invaders. For the moment, the two religions would have to live side-by-side.

As Cunval strode noisily through the long grass beside a pebble-strewn beach, his thoughts were jolted into focus by the faint call of a child in distress. Had he been mistaken? Was it children at play? Could it be the sound of the next rapids? He forced his way through to the water's edge and ran along the shingle. There it was again, a child screaming for help. Rushing forward, he could now see a figure splashing in the river near the far bank. He shrugged off his backpack and dropped his staff, at the same time jumping and wading through the water. A boy was almost face down in the river, whilst hanging on to some alder roots. Cunval had to dive and swim the last few yards. The boy looked up, terror on his face, and it was only then that Cunval could see that he was trying to pull up another child, a little girl, whose face was barely above the water as she gurgled and swallowed. The water was swirling above Cunval's waist as he grabbed for the huge tangle of roots that bounced with his weight. He clutched at the girl's shoulders but she was stuck, her face would hardly come above the dark water.

"Her foot is wedged," shouted the boy. "She's caught in the roots."

Cunval immediately dived downwards and felt for her foot. He opened his eyes under the freezing water, something he had never done before, and could see the child's foot pushed down through a tangle of large roots. In a moment, he put both feet against the roots and yanked upwards with his hands. He saw her leg come free as the boy pulled her clear, and, gasping for breath, they all clambered up the bank and onto the grass. The girl was crying and choking when Cunval turned her over and pressed into her back. The mixture of coughing and fighting for breath was followed by quick gasps. She was going to be all right.

"Oh, thank you, God. Thank you." Cunval pulled the girl to his chest and rocked her, at the same time, he rubbed the boy's back vigorously. "It's going to be all right. We must get you into dry clothes. Where do you live? Where's your mother?"

"It was Rees's fault," sobbed the girl. "He was fooling around, and pushed me."

The boy tried to express his innocence, but Cunval smiled

and laughed with relief.

"You're safe, my babies."

"I'm not a baby," protested the girl. "I'm ten."

"Sorry, sorry. Now, let me get you home. Which way do we go?"

All three staggered to their feet and set off upstream, Cunval with his arm around the little girl.

"You were very brave, both of you. What are your names?"

"I'm Rees. I'm twelve, and this is Olwen. She's always falling over."

Olwen had given up protesting, the cold water must have affected her more than Cunval thought. He must get her to a fire.

It was not far to the wooden palisade of the farmstead. They ran through the gate and past various thatched, scruffy buildings. The hall house was high, with mud walls and a roof black with years of smoke. First, the dogs barked, and then women came from all directions, shrieking and shouting out orders. They all bustled Cunval and the little ones into the hall, where they crouched at the central fire, the women at the same time removing the children's clothes.

"What happened? "Rees and Olwen's mother was wrapping them in a large cow's hide, held open to the warm fire. They would soon be recovered.

"It was an accident," explained Olwen. "The bank gave away and I fell into the river. I just got wet, that's all."

It was obvious to Cunval that the children were afraid of being scolded, so they were trying to make light of the near-tragic incident. Then, the women seemed to notice Cunval for the first time. He nodded in agreement.

"Yes, I just happened to be walking up the river bank and…"

"Give the children some broth."

A large metal cauldron was hanging over the fire. Cunval realised then that he, too, was thirsty and hungry.

Shadows from the doorway caused Cunval to look around. He could not see clearly, as the last rays of evening sunshine pierced the interior gloom, but there were many male voices.

Several big men, wearing leather tunics that made them look fearsome, strode across the clay floor to the fire. The women glossed over the incident of the children and the men laughed. The oldest man, tall and stout and with a matted grey beard, simply growled. He slumped into a low couch by the fire; it creaked under his weight. Cunval timidly wrapped his wet clothes tightly around his body, trying to look insignificant. A dead deer was thrown onto the floor, its throat cut and its tongue protruding. Cunval shuddered.

"This man helped us, Grandad," said Rees. Yarl Brockvael, for it was he, saw the shrivelled figure of Cunval for the first time. He glanced down at the priest's habit and howled with rage.

"The damned priest. I knew it. As soon as he gets near the place, there's trouble."

Cunval jumped up. "May I introduce myself, sire," he stuttered. "My name is Cunval. Bishop Dyfrig has sent me here to …

"Brochvael snorted. "I know why you are here. You're going to try to convert us to this Christian rubbish."

All the men burst out laughing and looked down on

Cunval's frail form.

"If he's been in the river, give him some broth." A strong young man, dressed in furs and leather, and with a sword at his belt, stepped forward. He was obviously a war-leader. The others made way for him, as Rees's mother ladled some broth into a bowl. "Give him a dry cloak, and get those clothes off him."

Cunval was grateful, for he now felt quite faint. He knew that the soldier did not like him, despite his hospitality. He was undoubtedly Brockvael's son.

Before he could protest, several women started pulling off his tunic, exposing his skinny body. His undergarment was whipped off and he nearly collapsed with shame; never again could he be taken seriously as a priest. He covered his private parts with one hand and clasped the small copper cross hanging from his neck with the other. The Yarl led the laughter at Cunval's embarrassment, and he was thrown a fur-skin cloak.

The men started relating stories of the day's hunting as Cunval once more settled on the floor. The fur around his shoulders was sheer luxury. He was handed a bowl. After a few sips at its contents, Cunval retched and the broth sprayed onto the edge of the fire. "It's meat," he gasped. "I can't eat it. I can't."

"Get him out of here," ordered Brockvael. "Put him in with the animals, tonight." Rees and Olwen winced, for Cunval seemed so child-like.

"My pack," cried Cunval. "I've lost my backpack and all my belongings." He put his hands to his head in sheer panic and looked at the doorway." It's on the riverbank, I remember now. Do excuse me. I'll be back soon. I'll do some work later."

As he ran out of the door, the men shook their heads in disbelief. This novice priest was going to be a huge nuisance.

There was still enough daylight for Cunval to find his way and stride back down-river, clutching the cloak tightly around him. He felt utterly miserable; he had made a complete mess of his first meeting with the clan and, if he had lost his precious belongings, he was in serious trouble. Arriving at the rescue spot, Cunval looked downstream to the shallower rapids, in order see where best to cross. He then became aware of a motionless figure on the opposite bank. An old man stood looking at him.

"Are you the priest?" he shouted above the noise of the river. "I've got your back-pack and your staff. I kept them safe for you, Father."

This was the first time that Cunval had been called Father.

"Oh, thank you, thank you! I was so worried. You're most kind." Cunval started to wade across, holding the cloak clear of the water. He dare not stumble and get wet again.

"I saw what happened, Father. I was up in the field, and, by the time I got down here, you were all off to the hall. Are the children all right?"

Cunval, wheezing, could only nod as the old man grasped his outstretched hand. He then led him to the discarded pack, which was still lying where Cunval had shed it.

"I was afraid my pack and belongings would be lost." Cunval stooped as the old man helped him on with the heavy load.

"I'm a Christian, you know. There's only me and my dear wife left. You know what happened to the rest, don't you?"

Cunval nodded and clasped the old man's hands. "I can't tell you how happy I am to meet you. God bless you!"

The old man picked up Cunval's staff, which had a cross carved in the top.

"Stay in our house, Father. We have bread," he said.

It was only at this point that Cunval realised how providence had shone upon him. He had surely been chosen to be in this place and at this time. He clasped the old man's hands. The riverside pathway felt good under his wet, stockinged feet, but his clogs now belonged to the river.

chapter 3

"They call me Henbut," said the old man, as he led the way up-river. "My wife and I have a small house in the enclosure. Brockvael does not often allow us into his Hall; he hates Christians, you know. Blames them for everything."

"Yes, I think it's going to be difficult for me, Henbut. I'm going to need your help. I'll have to approach Brockvael in the morning, to ask him where he wants me to work. Bishop Dyfrig said that I would be given a piece of ground of my own, so that I can start a Christian cemetery. Do you think that Brockvael will co-operate?"

"Eventually, perhaps."

They arrived at a spot on the riverbank opposite the hall. In the gloom, Cunval could see the high wooden palisade enclosing the farm buildings and roundhouses; all of the habitations seemed to have smoke drifting through their thatched roofs. The Hall dominated the central area, and it was all very depressing to Cunval, to think that they still worshipped pagan gods. He wondered if he would even be allowed to mention Jesus.

"Look at that bridge!" Cunval stopped and stared at the huge wooden construction that spanned a narrow point in the river. Two long tree trunks were wedged side by side between alder clumps on either bank; a thick rope was looped above this walkway, with thinner ropes lashed downwards. These ropes, in turn, held fast a smooth handrail; it all looked very safe.

"Follow me," said Henbut. Shorter trunks led from the bank to the main bridge, and Cunval could see that the tops of the trunks had been axed off level, and a long packing piece was inserted between them, to give a flat walkway. Having been trained in carpentry, Cunval had to admire this lovely bridge; it was a work of art. He was not to know that it had been mostly built by Durwit, the pagan priest of the district.

Cunval entered the enclosure for the second time that day; he felt claustrophobic in the gloom and pulled the borrowed fur cloak tightly around his waist. There were planked walkways between the buildings, to keep one's feet out of the mud. Cunval could see that the dogs were fond of Henbut and they whined in greeting.

"I must go into the Hall for my robe. I hope they haven't thrown it on the fire." Cunval dropped off his rucksack outside the doorway, nodded meekly to Henbut and entered. Rees's mother was the first to notice him and beckoned him to the fire.

"Your robe is drying. Come back for it in the morning. You can keep the cloak for now." The smile on her face told Cunval that she was sympathetic towards him and he was glad. The general chatter ceased briefly, as the men looked round at the priest.

Brockvael lay back on his couch, with a woman seated on either side of him. A young woman was holding his meat, a leg of some poor animal, and the older woman held up a wooden mug of what looked like beer. Cunval avoided his gaze and thanked Rees' mother. Rees and his sister, who had been seated by the fire, jumped up and clasped Cunval's hands.

"We'll show you the woods and the moor tomorrow," they sang out together. "What's your name?"

"Cunval. Well thank you, but I must work in the morning."

Brockvael burped loudly as Cunval turned towards the door. He suddenly felt very weary and very hungry. Henbut carried the haversack to his house.

"My wife, Mair!" said Henbut proudly. An upright, elderly lady came to the doorway, her grey hair tied back. She smiled a warm welcome and took Cunval's hand.

"This is the priest, my dear. He arrived today."

"Yes, I heard all about it. You saved the little girl's life, Father. The women have been talking. We're so glad that you've come to us; we'll do everything we can to help you."

Cunval made the sign of the cross and limped through the doorway. A central hearth and some small oil lamps gave off a dim light. He was aware of several people to the rear of the room.

"These are some of the labourers, Father. We share this house, as you can see. Please sit down. I'll serve you some of our fish stew; there aren't many vegetables at this time of the year, I'm afraid."

Cunval raised his hand in greeting to the men, who were seated on a bench near the fire, and thirstily drank a large jug of spring water. He was handed a steaming dish.

"This fish stew is lovely, Mair. I can taste the herbs. And the bread and butter is delicious."

"We have plenty of spare clothes, Father. Now, let me

tend to your poor feet. Mair led Cunval to a bowl of warm, salted water, where she bathed his feet with great care. After drying them and massaging in some ointment, Mair rolled a pair of warm bed-socks onto his feet. The labourers looked on bemused, for they had not seen such hospitality before.

Cunval was reminded of the hermits of the Egyptian desert, whose humility and respect for travellers was renowned. They would always wash and tend the feet of visitors and they had, above all else, a reputation for being gentle and humble, and considered themselves no better than any sinners. The stories and teachings of the early Christian fathers had been an inspiration to all the pupils of Caerleon.

Cunval was then aware of being helped to a raised bunk, away from the door. Henbut and his wife covered him with hides, and he quickly fell into a deep sleep.

chapter 4

Cunval woke with a start. He had been dreaming that Brockvael and his sons were trying to drown him. They were going to make it look like an accident; he threshed about in the river, his tunic full of large stones.

"Ah, you're awake, Father!" Henbut's wife was working at the hearth. "You have slept well. I have some rosehip tea for you, and bread and honey."

"I must have been dreaming. It's late." Cunval had slept soundly between dreams and now felt quite refreshed. "This is very kind of you, Mair."

"You look much better. The men have gone to the fields. It will be dry again today, and they expect to start ploughing. If you are going to see Brockvael, he is not out of bed yet. I hope you're not going to be shocked to know that he has two wives."

"Two wives! That's terrible."

Cunval remembered the two women on the couch. Mair proceeded to tell Cunval all he needed to know of Brockvael's estate. They chatted for some time, until another woman came to the doorway with Cunval's dry robe and a thick pair of woollen stockings. Cunval thanked her warmly. After a whispered conversation with her visitor, Mair suggested that it was time for Cunval to go to the Hall.

The barking dogs brought the older wife to the Hall entrance. She beckoned Cunval to the fireplace and motioned for him to sit on a low stool.

"I'm Gwenhaen," she announced, "Is your robe dry?" Just then, a stirring opposite the fireplace drew Cunval's attention. The whole Hall was divided by partitioning into various sleeping quarters. It was customary for an extended family to sleep together within the Hall, with the dogs on guard just outside. As Cunval peered across the fire, a young woman sat up from the bedclothes; she was naked to the waist. Cunval immediately turned around and stared at the floor. He had never seen a naked woman before and the blood rushed to his neck. It seemed like an age before he heard a growling noise from Brockvael.

"Arghh! The priest." A slurping noise could only have been Brockvael drinking from a bowl. "I suppose you want some land. That damn bishop of yours accosted me when I was in Caerleon last. He's a crafty devil, and made me promise to give some, when the King was present to hear me."

Cunval felt a surge of relief. A prod on the shoulder from the old wife meant that Cunval should now face the Yarl.

"Thank you so much, sire. I promise to work hard, and I'll be no bother to you. It means so much to me, to have a Christian cemetery and a sanctuary."

The naked woman was now dressed. Cunval tried to avoid looking at her. She was very pretty, with long dark hair, and was only in her twenties.

Brockvael laughed loudly.

"You haven't seen the land yet, priest. Still, you like hard work, you say. There's a small spring across the river, up on the moor, but it dries up in a hot summer. You can have as much of that ground as you like, but you'll need good fences."

Cunval was elated and he could feel that Gwenhaen, the older wife, was happy for him. "Where do you want me to work, sire?"

"Better see Henbut. He's the only one with any sense, even if he is a stupid Christian. Off, now."

As Cunval bowed in thanks, he heard the sound of children's voices. Rees, his sister and four other children were entering the Hall. They had obviously come to see Cunval, for he was soon surrounded by laughing youngsters, pulling at his robe and looking intently into his face. This was a joyous moment; he had an affinity with boisterous youngsters. His time as a teacher had prepared him well.

Rees ran over to Brockvael, who was struggling to get to his feet.

"Grandad, can we show Cunval the woods?" Rees helped Brockvael to his feet; he was obviously a favourite with the old man and could cajole Brockvael into anything. Cunval had learnt that Rees's father, Brockvael's eldest son, had been killed in a battle with the Saxons just before Olwen was born. The children of the settlement, as with any Celtic community, were given much freedom and were encouraged to develop in their own way. The tougher boys were expected to become soldiers; in fact, Cunval's own elder brother was a soldier and had seen many battles. Cunval had met him several times in Caerleon and had been horrified at the war stories. The Saxons in the east were greatly feared. They had taken many captives during their invasions, and every tenth captive was sacrificed to the god Woden. The rest were put to abject slavery.

Cunval tried not to think of all this violence, but he knew that, without Brockvael and his warriors, his own civilised life would end.

"Show him the spring on the moor, then, but he must be at work in the fields tomorrow." Perhaps Brockvael's bark was worse than his bite, thought Cunval. Gwenhaen signalled for them all to retreat quickly.

Rees had his own dog, Hawk. The other boys were slightly younger, and looked forward to having their own dogs, too, next year. As they had done with most animals, the Romans had crossed their own breeds of dog with that of the Celts, over hundreds of years. The British winters could be hard, and Cunval knew that there was a fine balance between the hardy Celtic bloodlines and the nimble Mediterranean breeds. The crossbreeding of horses was a passion with the tribes, and the exchange of horses and cattle as gifts was paramount to tribal unity. Cunval's old monastery at Caerleon had famous herds of cattle, sheep and goats; and bred fowls and ducks in great numbers, for the King to hand out to his Yarls and their estates.

"To the bridge, to the bridge, men," shouted Rees.

Everybody lined up, Cunval was ordered to follow the boys, and the girls trailed behind. The dogs that were still tethered under the overhanging eaves of the roofs barked furiously as they were left behind. Cunval had a hard job keeping up; his ankles were stiff from the last few days of hiking. For the first time, he felt he could relax. He had now met the clan, it had partly accepted him, and he had been given land; perhaps things would all work out as he settled in. He was already surrounded by a potential young flock, and there was no such thing as bad children.

The bridge shook and trembled as the many feet stamped across the planking, the boys teasing the girls, to show them that they were firmly in charge. The river looked so beautiful in the morning sun, and they all stopped on the bridge to watch two men fishing in a deep pool below. They were on a moored tree-trunk canoe, peering down into the clear cold water, each with a long spear. Cunval knew that the ends of the spears would have several barbs, and a fine rope would be tied securely to the shaft. The spring salmon were starting to run and there would be no shortage of fish from now on.

Hawk had scampered gingerly across the swaying bridge, and had immediately started his hunting pattern, sniffing into bushes and holes. Hunting was the main pastime of any community, and the children sometimes brought back a hare or a small deer.

"Up the hill, men," ordered Rees. "We'll show Cunval his spring."

As they all trekked up a well-used pathway, Cunval darkly recalled that, on his journey from Caerleon, there had been several clear springs. Each spring had its own Celtic god, or goddess, and they were sacred places to the pagans.

"Not far now, men!" shouted Rees, as they neared the brow of a low hill.

A small gulley with water trickling downhill indicated a meagre spring. The boys pulled back the low bushes to reveal a shallow pool where water could be collected.

"It's not much," shrugged Rees. The children all looked at Cunval sympathetically.

"It's perfect, Rees. I don't want anything too much. I can dig it out a bit."

The water was crystal clear and ran over a bed of bright pebbles. Cunval would build it into a proper well. He glanced around at the landscape. They were standing on a large plateau with scattered daffodils, scrub, gorse and small trees. As a matter of course, they put sprigs of greenery into their hair. The pathway just below them ran on up to moor land that appeared to go on forever. The only land under cultivation was around the settlement, where the general slope was to the south.

Olwen had held Cunval's hand, hoping that he wouldn't be too disappointed with his plot of land. She knew that he was meant to live on his own, away from the Hall. Cunval smiled down at her. He could already picture his very own llan, a stone-walled enclosure with a high wooden cross, just like Tidiog's. First, he had to win the respect of the clan.

"Let's show you the moors, Cunval," offered Rees.

The boys charged off, howling war-cries. They came to some grazing cattle, mostly black and with long horns. The cattle looked up at them dispassionately, more concerned with grazing on the heather tips and the little grass that was showing. Together with the wild deer, they had long since stripped the low parts of the few trees that had managed to survive on the moor.

The sky was clear and blue; the only sound was the screeching from a pair of buzzards who were trying to get rid of last year's reluctant youngster. Cunval loved his new home and, to the amusement of the children, started singing.

chapter 5

The moor stretched far to the east. It was a wild and desolate place and not somewhere to be caught in bad weather, but with the children on a sunny day, for Cunval, it was paradise. The children knew the pathways so well and were pleased to show off to Cunval. A small group of fallow deer jumped up from their resting-place in the heather. Rees set Hawk after them, but the dog was too low down to see over the heather and soon lost the scent.

"We need spears for hunting," ordered Rees. "Let's go down to the woods. I know a good place."

Rees was a born leader; they all wheeled to the left and made for the tree-line above the river. Rees was the only one with a knife, which he kept in a sheath on his belt; it had a bone handle and was very sharp.

"This hazel is the straightest, men. You bend them over and I'll cut. Do you want a spear, Cunval?"

"No thank you. I couldn't kill an animal, or bird, I'm afraid." Cunval was apologetic, but didn't mention fish, of course. "I think of them all as God's creatures."

"Which God?" asked one of the younger boys.

"There's only one God," replied Cunval.

"Where does he live?"

"Oh, ah, in heaven, everywhere."

The boy frowned. "Does he have a wife?"

"No, but he had a son, Jesus, who was killed by the

Romans, hundreds of years ago."

"Was there a battle?"

"Not exactly; well, sort of!"

The children had gathered around, even the dog seemed to be listening. This was a good chance to talk of Jesus, but with such a sensitive issue, Cunval felt quite inadequate.

Olwen looked up at Cunval's tonsure.

"Why are you so bald on the front part of your head? Are you from another tribe? Henbut told us that priests are good at telling stories. Tell us a story, Cunval."

Cunval remembered the parable of the Good Samaritan. He sat down on the bank and tried to make the story sound interesting. Thankfully, it seemed to meet with their approval.

"Does God have spirits in the trees?" Rees waved his half-finished spear towards the forest.

"No, there's only one Holy Spirit, and he's around you everywhere." The children looked around them.

"What about the river spirits? They look after the dead people in the big pool. What does God do with the dead people? Does he keep them in the sea?"

This was going too fast for Cunval. He knew something of the pagan funerary rights, with pools and lakes, but he had never witnessed such things.

"Well, what I'm hoping to do is set up a Christian cemetery, you see, near the spring. Then, if anyone who dies is a Christian, I'll bury them in a deep hole and say special prayers. Then their soul goes up to heaven."

"What's a soul?"

"A sort of spirit."

"Don't you burn dead people? Brockvael gets his

magician to burn the dead people, and then he puts their ashes into the deep pool, where they're safe for ever."

When Rees mentioned the word 'magician', Cunval was alarmed. He'd heard of ancient pagan rites, performed by druids and shamans, but he had only heard whispers of such a shaman in the Penhal district.

"I know, let's talk about trees. I see you have some beautiful trees in this wood. Do you know what they're all called? They've all got different jobs to do, you know."

The children shrugged. Cunval knew that he should be gentle when trying to spread the good word. His young pupils at Caerleon had always asked him where babies came from, knowing that he would turn bright red. For Cunval, that was a troublesome and perplexing subject.

"Do you know what this tree is?" Cunval put his arms around a large ash tree.

"Ash!" they all said together. "It's good for firewood."

"I use it to make beds, chairs and tables," said Cunval brightly. "I'm quite good at carpentry, you know."

"Will you make me a new bed?" asked Olwen.

Cunval laughed and nodded; he knew that they would all now want something or other made up. "I call ash trees the sentries of the wood," said Cunval. "That's because they're tall and straight and can see over all the other trees. Now, what about this tree?"

"Birch." said Olwen, looking upwards. "Alright for brooms and nasty medicines, not much else, though."

"I call them the dancers. Have you noticed how they dance in the breeze, with their silver trunks and long slender branches like hands?" Cunval waved his hands in imitation and the children followed suit. This was pleasing.

Cunval set off downhill. "Who do you think the singers of the forest and river bank are?"

Rees pre-empted Cunval's question. "The alder trees!"

"Very good. Have you noticed how they rub against one another sometimes and make a grating noise? Well, that's singing. Then there's the hazels; they're laughing and joking all the time; they can pop up anywhere."

"What about Brockvael? Which tree does he look like?"

The gang burst out laughing and Cunval laughed too. They all looked around and pointed at a very old lime tree. It had been pollarded in ancient times, to serve as a boundary marker, and it had become gnarled and twisted, with great holes in its huge trunk.

"You should have more respect for the Yarl," scolded Cunval, with a wagging finger. However, the boys were now pointing to a young, slender yew tree, and whispering urgently. Being evergreen, its cone-shaped top stood out amongst the other woodland trees that had not yet burst into spring leaf. When Cunval looked across at the top-heavy yew, they all fell about on the ground. Cunval was secretly pleased at this personal joke, even though he wasn't sure what the joke was. He felt as if he was going to be one of the gang.

"I hope you realise that the trees are listening to you and discussing your disrespectful mockery." The children waited for Cunval to continue. "They all have their roots touching underground, you know. That's how they hold hands and talk; and the news that we humans are here has just spread right throughout the wood. Well, what do you think of that?"

The children looked at the ground and lifted their feet

one at a time, whilst Cunval strolled on downhill, whistling. They were soon charging after him, the dead leaves scattering under the stampede.

"Let's show Cunval the deep pool with the spirits. It's a bit spooky. Wait, there's a spring just ahead. Let's have a drink first." Rees, as usual, led the way.

Cunval, out of morbid curiosity, wanted to see the pagan pool. He knew that any attempt to convert the clan to Christianity was going to be difficult and, possibly, dangerous. They soon came to a bubbling spring and thirstily scooped up the cold, pure water that cascaded over the mossy rocks.

"All water comes from the Earth Mother, you know."

Cunval looked up inquisitively at Olwen's statement. "Don't you think that she's God's wife?"

"Well, in a way, I suppose. You see, Olwen, God is the creator of everything. He made the earth, and the heavens, and the stars."

"It must have taken him a long time. Who helped him, Cunval?"

Cunval was lost for words; the children were making it very difficult for him. Luckily, Rees had a theory to explain the matter.

"Well, I think that God is the sun, and the moon is his wife, and all the stars are their children."

The other children frowned and nodded, thoughtfully. "And then, when a star comes down to earth, a baby is born!"

They all thought that was a good explanation, and Cunval decided not to interfere at this stage. He wondered how they would react to the story of Adam and Eve.

"Let's practice throwing our spears."

One of the boys stepped forward and, with great dexterity, hurled his spear downhill at a dead elm tree. One by one, the other children followed suit. Even the two smaller girls seemed to be adept at this serious game.

"That's very good," said Cunval, who was tempted to have a go himself. "I bet the Saxons would never stand a chance in a battle with you."

After a mad chase through the wood and towards the river, they arrived at a pathway high above the pool. The water looked dark and deep where it entered through the neck of the pool and slowly swirled around the bank below them. The eddy on the far bank was surmounted by a large natural rock, which Cunval knew immediately would be a focal point for any pagan ceremonies. The small stream, which emanated from the spring where they had stopped to drink, cascaded over an outcrop and into the lower section of the pool. They all sat on the bank; there was no doubt this was a place of great beauty. Cunval could imagine this spot on a summer evening, later in the year.

"Nobody is allowed near the pool, Cunval," warned Rees. "All canoes have to be carried along the bank, you know. And there's a huge pike in there, and giant rats." He continued, "Do you see the channels and ponds downstream? They are for catching eels, Cunval. Do you like eels?"

"Yes, Rees. Eels are very nice, but I catch mine with an eel trap, left overnight. Have you seen an eel trap?"

This caused great excitement. Cunval tried to explain, but that was just not good enough for the children, who wanted to see one. With the help of Rees' knife, Cunval set to work. He cut and bent hazel whips to form a barrel-shaped body to the trap, while the boys cut down a suitable elm branch. Leaving a forked end to the branch, Cunval proceeded to notch the supple bark at the base. He was able to peel it off in strips the full length of the branch, and this made suitable bindings. After showing the girls how to weave the bindings in and out of the hazel whips, he left them to it. The boys watched with great interest as Cunval firstly made up a detachable end to the trap, and then formed a funnel-shaped entrance section complete with a hole. This he was able to insert into the body of the trap, at the same time binding on a handle for easy carrying. Before finally tying the handle, he slipped the fork of the elm branch through it and then stood up. With the branch over his shoulder and the trap swinging loosely behind him, Cunval posed with a smug grin.

"Phew!" Rees was very taken with this new invention. "How do you get the eels to go through the hole?" He paused and thought for a moment, then said, "I know. I know. You put something dead in there first, right?"

"Exactly, and the bindings will let the water through but not a good size eel, right?"

"Let's go down towards the bridge," said Rees in reply. "I know a good place where there must be lots of eels." They trouped off, in anticipation of some sport.

chapter 6

By the time they arrived at the chosen spot, Cunval needed to sit down for a while.

"Now, we want worms or grubs to catch some minnows."

The children delved under stones and leaf-mould whilst Cunval opened up the end of the trap.

"Who can chop them up?"

Cunval wished to avoid this job, but Rees enthusiastically cut up the small worms on a flat stone.

"That's it, now wrap them up in a leaf and pop them into the trap."

Cunval lowered the trap on the end of the elm stick into some shallow water, where they could all watch. Soon, a shoal of minnows had congregated around the trap.

"There," whispered Olwen. "I think some fish went into the funnel!"

Cunval waited a while, then carefully raised up the trap, funnel end first. The river water filtered out of the trap when Cunval swung it onto the bank and opened the blank end.

"Three. Three!" Olwen was delighted.

"Now," Cunval grimaced. "Who is going to cut up the poor minnows?"

Rees needed no encouragement. He was the acknowledged expert with his knife. "Shall I put them into the trap now?" Rees scraped up the sticky mess from the flat stone. Cunval kept the trap at arm's length while he tied up the end. "By here!" Rees pointed. "This is the spot."

"I'll try and get it close to the roots." Cunval lowered the trap into a deep hole near the bank and wedged the elm branch into the alder roots just above the water.

"How long will it be, Cunval?" Olwen put her hand on his shoulder and peered into the dark water.

"It should be left overnight, really," replied Cunval, "but we can have a look in a while, perhaps." The harassed priest was now glad just to sit down and rest his feet. Rees' dog felt the same way.

"I know, tell us another story," suggested one of the boys. "Do you know any stories about soldiers?"

Cunval thought for a while; he wanted to be gentle with the children. Their upbringing had encompassed the violence and superstition of the Celtic and Roman gods, and he wanted the children to ask about his God and Jesus, so that he could tell them about Christian beliefs rather than to try to convince them that their own spirit world was evil.

"There was a soldier-prince called Illtyd," whispered Cunval. The children leaned forward. "He had been very brave in battle against the Saxons and, at the age of only twenty-five, he became a general." The two girls cuddled up to Cunval; they loved stories. "In one battle, the Saxons killed his horse with a lance, and his best friend had his arm cut off, and another friend was pushed off a cliff." Cunval thought he would embellish the story with a few bloodthirsty details. "Anyway, the day arrived when Illtyd got fed up with all the wars and the killing, and he went hunting alone in the woods. Soon, he was chasing a noble young stag."

"Did he kill the Saxon who speared his horse?" Rees wanted even more detail.

"Not sure," replied Cunval. "I think the Saxon ran off. In the wood, he eventually came to an old hermit's hovel, and the stag was lying down by his door, exhausted. Illtyd was about to kill it with his spear when the hermit stood in the way and begged for the poor deer's life. Illtyd just could not understand how anyone could plead for the life of an animal. He dropped his spear and sat down with the hermit, who offered him a mug of milk."

"Did the stag run off then?"

"Well, no. That's the funny thing; the stag licked Illtyd's hand." The girls gasped. "The old hermit explained that he, too, had once been a soldier and, eventually, he could bear that way of life no longer. So, he lived in the woods for the rest of his life, and the thing that gave him most happiness was talking to travellers."

"What did he eat?"

"Nuts, berries, fish stew; he grew vegetables and corn in a little field, and he was always happy. Anyway, Illtyd, listening to the old man, suddenly felt a strange peace come over him and he started to cry." The girls breathed in and Cunval paused. "Then, a dove flew onto Illtyd's shoulder."

"A dove!" shrieked Olwen. "What happened then?"

"Well, the old man comforted Illtyd because he knew that from then on he would never want to harm anybody ever again. Then the hermit advised Illtyd to go to a nearby monastery, where they would allow him to stay the night."

"And did the deer show him the way?" Olwen was so

glad that the young stag had survived.

"Umm, yes, I think you're probably right, Olwen." Cunval then proceeded to relate how Illtyd stayed with the monks for a long time and eventually became a priest. This gave Cunval a chance to explain what a monastery was and how they were all dedicated to the love of God and mankind.

"Did Illtyd have an eel trap?"

"Yes, I expect so."

"Was the monastery near a river?"

"Yes, and they would always give food and shelter to hungry travellers."

"Did the Saxons try and kill them?" enquired Rees.

"No, they were well inland."

"And did the King's soldiers protect them?" This was a pointed question and Cunval nodded vaguely.

"Let's see if we've caught any eels!" Cunval jumped up followed by the children and they all peered into the water. "I doubt if the eels are about during the day," mused Cunval. "They usually come out at night." He carefully lifted the trap and swung it over the bank onto a sandy patch. They all gathered round, as the end was untied. Two small crayfish had squeezed into the trap and now dropped onto the sand. The children laughed as Rees picked them up.

"They're too small to eat. I know, let's use them as bait for the eels!"

"Oh, no," groaned Cunval, as Rees placed them on a rock, and expertly crushed them with a stone. "There, now tie up the end again, Cunval," he said.

"Perhaps, we can leave it till the morning." Cunval allowed Rees to lower the trap back into place, and soon they were all moving downstream to the bridge.

Crossing the bridge turned into a game of dare for the boys, but Hawk, wisely, decided it was safer to wade across the river on his four legs. Then, there was one last throw of the spears toward the gate before the smell of food drew them all to the Hall entrance. The men and dogs had gone off hunting, leaving the women to prepare the morning's fresh salmon. They were also busy making new clothes and stacking the firewood. Everybody was glad to see the children back safely and noted well that they were happy and excited. Of course, they all tried to talk at once, explaining Cunval's wisdom of the trees, and his storytelling.

"The children showed me around the woods and the moor," said Cunval. "I was delighted with my patch of ground, you know. It has its own spring, and I know it will be ideal for growing vegetables."

Rees and Olwen's mother nodded approval. This was good; it meant that Cunval was going to be accepted by the families.

"My name is Anhared," she offered. "You can call me that."

Cunval formally thanked her and bowed. The other women giggled. Benches were pulled forward for the children to sit on and they were all handed bowls of stew, with freshly baked bread. Cunval gratefully took his bowl with a warm chunk of bread and a beverage made of pine tips and mint.

Cunval whispered a prayer in Latin, and Olwen glanced at him inquisitively. Cunval smiled back.

The children then related Cunval's invention of the eel trap. They were all going to inspect the trap in the morning.

"It wasn't really my invention," Cunval explained to

Anhared. "Anyway, I must be off to the fields now, they'll need every help if the ploughing has started." The children looked disappointed. "Thank you so much for the refreshment."

They all waved goodbye as Cunval made for the doorway and strode off. He was conscious of not imposing too much on the day-to-day running of the community.

He changed into some boots that Mair had given him, before setting off for the far fields where two teams of oxen were ploughing the still wet soil. Henbut and a labourer were following one of the ploughs, breaking up the sticky clay furrows with hoes.

"Good afternoon," shouted Cunval. "Forgive me for not coming out earlier. Brockvael has given me some land, and the children have been showing me the woods."

Henbut rested on his hoe and smiled.

"I'm glad, Father. In any case, you should rest for a day after your long journey here. We have all April to plough and prepare the fields, and these fine fellows enjoy it so much. Look at them." The labourers, who had all stopped work to examine Cunval, groaned in unison, with mock signs of fatigue.

"This man be a Roman slave-driver," said the nearest labourer, pointing an accusing finger at Henbut. His colleagues laughed loudly. "I dare say we'll be on the funeral pyre long before him."

"His names is Cam," sighed Henbut.

Cunval laughed with them. He was glad to know that they all worked together in good heart. Humour was an important part of life for the farming community; work was always hard, and famine or pestilence could always be just around the corner.

Aware that the labourers were inspecting him, Cunval walked over to the horses and spoke to them softly. He realised that his skinny legs and slender hands were amusing to the tough workmen.

"Ere. Why does Henbut call you 'Father'? You're not his father."

"No, of course I'm not. It's just a title." Cunval was not used to being addressed as 'Father', and hoped that it would not cause confusion or resentment.

He turned to Henbut. "Look, it may be best if you all call me Cunval."

"That's fine by me, Father, I mean Cunval." Henbut could also see the difficulties.

They all went back to work and were surprised at Cunval's knowledge of the land. He kept going all afternoon. Hard work was enjoyable to Cunval, if the result was to the benefit of his fellow man.

On the way home with the horses, they chatted like old friends.

"I have a good selection of seeds in my back-pack," said Cunval, "I'll gladly share them with you. I've got special onion seed from our monastery, and turnips, carrots, peas, cucumber, celery, cabbage." He nodded his head as he tried to remember each item. "Oh, and yes, I've got some vine cuttings and raspberries."

"What you talking about? I've never heard of that lot!" Cam was the chief labourer and the village joker.

"You'll see, when I get my garden together," laughed Cunval.

The first day had worked out well and the evening in

Henbut's house was going to cement the new relationships. After bathing in the cold river, Cunval inspected his poor feet. Mair produced some ointment and clean woollen socks. Later, with a full stomach and a warm bed, sleep was instant and deep.

chapter 7

A light drizzle had upset the morning plan for ploughing, and Henbut ordered a session of firewood-chopping in the large barn. Cunval offered to clean out the pigs; he was determined to make himself popular and, in any case, he wanted to reduce the awful smell by burying the spoil in the main compost heap. The children had gleefully called in to announce that the trap had caught a large eel, and they were going to have it for supper, but the smell of Cunval's work soon caused then to run off.

It was still drizzling at mid-day.

"That's enough for today, Cunval. We can manage the rest." Henbut wanted Cunval to have some time to spend with his new enclosure. "Here, I expect you'll need a hoe." Henbut had been reading Cunval's thoughts.

Eagerly, Cunval set off for the shallow ford down-river. He felt that he needed some time on his own, to take stock, and going through the enclosure might mean attracting the children. His new patch of ground beckoned him. He scrambled up the hillside to the spring and set about clearing the undergrowth. He would need his small axe next time, to clear the bigger trees.

He paced out his new cemetery and put in marker sticks. The enclosure, which would eventually contain a consecrated cemetery, was pretty well circular, and left another flat area that would be suitable for his garden. The smaller trees he could pull out of the damp ground well enough and he set all the debris aside to dry out for kindling wood.

Above the area that he was working on, there was a steep bank and crag complete with a scree of sandstone. With the woodland all around, this would make a lovely suntrap, but he knew that the biggest threat to his garden would be from the farm animals and the wild deer; he would need high fencing and a scarecrow to deter them.

Pulling down the rubble of the scree, he started to pick out suitable stones. He would need a stone platform for his hut, so he piled up suitable material at the rear of the enclosure.

After digging out a hole at the source of the spring, he stood back to rest and watched the water gradually build up. He then took off his cross and thong and hung it on a twig over the new pool; it danced back and fore, glinting in the sunlight.

Cunval noted with satisfaction that there was hard clay below the turf line. This meant that he could channel the water through the enclosure and into the garden area. This was all working out very well.

The sun had now reappeared and Cunval's damp tunic was steaming. He felt the next job was to prepare the area of his garden ready for digging. First, it was necessary to clear the ground, so he set to with the hoe. He expected this job to take weeks, depending on how much time he was given. The important thing was to turn the soil over while it was still damp.

Cunval was methodical in everything he did. The turf was stacked in a heap under the bank; this was the start of his compost heap. He would collect leaf-mould and loose soil from the woodland to dig in, and he would even carry baskets of old manure up the hillside.

It was essential to rest now and again. Cunval knew that he must not strain his back. The spring-water had now cleared and was delicious to taste. An early-leafing quickthorn bush provided him with some nutritious shoots to nibble. He lined the bottom and the sides of the pool with flat pieces of stone, and, whilst hoeing, he could not stop glancing with pride at his new creation. If the spring was going to be a holy well, then it should have a dedication. His thoughts had been going back to his monastery. He could not really name the well after any of his former masters, and it would be too presumptuous to think of naming it after any of the old Christian saints. Anyway, there was no hurry.

He loved the sound of nature around him. This spot was going to be paradise. He thought of Henbut and Mair coming to visit him on a Sunday evening for prayers; perhaps, some of the labourers would join his congregation. Men of the land were the most likely to see the true path. There were also the people who lived on the outlying farms. Some of them had been quite familiar with Christianity, when the previous priest had had a church at the old settlement, five miles up-river.

Cunval sat and looked upstream, contemplating the story of the lost church. About twelve years earlier, Bishop Dyfrig had sent a young priest, Dinabo, to the settlement upstream, where Brockvael's father, Morval, had retired. Brockvael, as the new Yarl, had built his own hall at Penhal and would have nothing to do with the new religion.

A sudden disease had swept through the old settlement and only a handful of farming families had survived. Everybody who was taken ill had gone to the church to die and, later, Brockvael had set fire to everything in the area. He blamed the whole thing on Christianity, with all its mumbo-jumbo; the superstitions of the old gods had since reigned supreme.

Few people had gone near the old settlement afterwards, apart from a visit by Bishop Dyfrig and his clergy, who came to perform a service. However, it was part of Cunval's mission to visit the site once he had settled in, and to see that the place was respectable. That would, he hoped, be soon.

For the moment, hunger was Cunval's his main concern. He toiled until almost dusk, when the air became chilly. There would be salmon for supper, with bread, butter, cheese and honey. It was time to go, and he sang all the way home.

Later in the evening, Henbut and the labourers were intrigued to know what was happening in the big city of Caerleon. Had Cunval ever seen the King and his court? Had the pirates raided the coast lately? The questions were endless.

Cunval's mind wandered. Holding his cross in his hand, which he often absentmindedly did, he suddenly felt a flash of inspiration.

"How stupid! How stupid! Why am I not thinking?"

The little cross had been given to him by a dear old lady, Evra, the mother of Bishop Dyfrig. She had journeyed, at the age of eighty, from her home in the north, declaring that she was dying and wanted to spend her remaining time near her son. The King insisted that she stay in his household, and, on occasion, Dyfrig had taken some of his pupils to see her and take afternoon broth. So the problem was solved, the spring would now be known as the Fountain of Evra, and dedicated to Bishop Dyfrig's blessed mother.

Cunval had seen little of the warrior Catvael and his band, who were proud soldiers and would never lower themselves to do manual work. Their main occupations in life seemed to be hunting, wrestling, training with weapons, grooming their horses and generally swaggering around the settlement. They took little interest in Cunval, and ignored him if they happened to be riding past his enclosure whilst Cunval was working. Even so, Cunval always smiled and waved politely.

Early one morning, Rees came excitedly to Cunval in the fields to say that Brockvael wanted to see him. He did not know why, but Cunval sensed that it could not be anything too horrible.

The Hall was dark as usual and there were no women to be seen. Cunval stood in front of the Yarl and spoke expectantly. "Sire?"

"Rees tells me that you want to go to the old settlement at Hentland."

Rees beamed at Cunval.

"Yes, sire. I need to see if everything is tidy, and, of course, say a few prayers."

"Bah! Now don't start that nonsense." Brockvael looked exasperated. "The thing is, my father's remains are there, and I haven't let anyone interfere with the place for ten years or more. I want Rees to see that sacred spot. He's my only grandson, and one day he'll be a great warrior. Do you understand my meaning?"

"Yes, sire." Cunval's duty was always to obey the king's representatives. This was a requirement of his faith, and today Brockvael certainly seemed to be in a condescending mood.

"We'll be quite safe, Grandfather. It will be a splendid expedition and Cunval will look after us." Rees was loving the thought of a new adventure.

"That's what I'm afraid of," grunted Brockvael, narrowing his eyes at Cunval. "If there's any trouble, I'll drown you."

"I'll, um, I'll… It will be all right, sire," Cunval blustered.

"I have a special job for you, priest. Nobody is allowed to touch the church building where the people died. My father's body was there when it was fired, but you're not part of our sacred religion, so I want you to look for our family amulet."

"Yes, sire. Where might it be?"

"My father was wearing it."

"You mean?"

"Exactly. Search in the rubble; and have respect for the bones." At this point, Brockvael brushed past Cunval and strode out of the door.

"You'll find it, Cunval," grimaced Rees, whilst Cunval rubbed his chin. He wasn't sure what he felt about this clear, but gruesome instruction.

The other children were waiting outside and, when Rees explained the important mission, they all whooped. They had never ventured so far before. The women hurriedly prepared food for them to take with them, while Hawk snapped playfully at everybody's heels. Cunval collected his staff from Henbut's house and told Mair of the journey.

chapter 8

Cunval decided to start the hike upstream on the left bank; this meant he could cut across the bend and avoid the big pool. Cattle and sheep grazed on the sloping ground that was divided into small fields, and the children explained that there would soon be calves and lambs. Then there would be fresh milk, to which the whole community was looking forward.

There was a delay while Rees cut new spears. He ominously informed the party that there might be wolves up-river.

"Now don't be alarmed, children. There may be wolves, up in the hills," explained Cunval, "but they don't come anywhere near humans. They run the other way."

"What about big snakes?" joked Rees, who was determined to frighten the younger ones.

"They don't come out until the summer," countered Cunval.

Rees snorted as the younger ones pointed their fingers at him. The hike was a sheer pleasure. They saw an otter, an osprey, ducks, moorhens, geese; and water-voles seemed to be everywhere. Cunval showed them the animal spoor in the fresh sand at the river's edge. There was a guessing game at the names of the trees and the flowers. Olwen was quicker than Rees, who easily became bored.

A large badger's set created some apprehensive interest,

and the children carefully avoided it.

"That's where the spirits of the witches live," said Olwen. "I'm not going anywhere near it."

"No, no," replied Cunval. "The badgers are God's creatures; they do no harm. And there are no such things as witches or spirits." Cunval sat on the mound of earth, laughing.

"Wolf!" cried one of the smaller boys, pointing to a clump of bushes ahead. "I saw a wolf."

"Now then, now then," soothed Cunval. In fact, he thought he had seen something himself, but it certainly wasn't a wolf. He called Hawk, who was rolling about on a sandbank, and they walked towards the bushes together. Hawk sniffed and growled quietly as they approached. Cunval parted the ivy-clad branches with his staff and peered into various clumps. He could see no tracks, and Hawk lost interest; perhaps it was just the breeze.

Cunval shrugged his shoulders and the gang caught up. "I think it was a deer," he said solemnly. "I know, let's find a sunny spot by the river and have something to eat."

This seemed like a good idea and Olwen took charge, sharing out the boiled eggs, salt, bread and cheese. There was also some honey-cake, but when it emerged from Olwen's shoulder bag, it was in crumbly pieces and had to be carefully divided.

"We mustn't drink any river water," Cunval reminded the children. "I'm sure there will be a spring not far away."

After observing some of the interesting river life under large stones, they moved on, and, sure enough, came to a spring.

"Look! There are feathers and carved sticks in the

branches, and this spring has been built up with stones." Rees looked puzzled.

Cunval scratched his chin. Tokens at a spring meant that somebody in the vicinity was clinging to old pagan rites.

"I suppose that there's a farm near here," he mused. "I expect the people use this spring sometimes."

After another short hike, Cunval recognized the site of the old settlement. It had been built on a shelf above the river, the palisade was almost gone, and there were only slight mounds where the buildings had been. A little way on, Cunval could determine the remains of a circular stone wall and in the middle were the obvious remains of the church. The stone walls stood knee-high above the ground, and the interior was a mass of rubble, briars and nettles. He made the sign of the cross as he approached, but the children, who had been instructed not to enter the cemetery enclosure, stood well back.

Cunval stood for a while, nodding his head; he knew that Dinabo, the priest, had been a good man. Now, the site was gone forever, and Christianity had inadvertently shouldered the blame.

He realised that his task would take some time. He would need to clear the tangle of undergrowth and move the rubble in order to get down to the old floor level. The first thing was to get the children interested in a game while he worked. They virtually did this themselves by trying to guess which building had been where and making comparisons with their own settlement.

Cunval cleared the old doorway in the south wall and slashed at the briars with his staff. The interior had only been six paces by three paces, but he decided that he must work from the doorway inwards, and pile the rubble back behind him. As he used the corner of his tunic to grip the briars and pull them up by the roots, the task went smoothly. Clearing downwards, he soon got into a thick layer of black ash and then the stone-slabbed floor.

He wasn't surprised when he came to the first charred human bones. These held no fear for him; bones were merely the earthly remains of mortals. He hoped that, in due course, his own would be buried deep in hallowed ground, and not be thrown into the river. The rubble cleared surprisingly quickly and he judged from the various remains that there had been at least twelve bodies in the church when it had served as a funeral pyre. There was a lot of burnt pottery, suggesting that the sick and dying were given water, probably by the priest. One or two trinkets came to light and Cunval replaced these in the ash. He would certainly be lucky to find the amulet. Perhaps Brockvael's father, Morval, had not even died in the church.

After an hour, he checked on the children; the sounds of their play told him that they were having fun, so he shouted apologies for the delay.

"I have strict orders from Brockvael," he explained. "So, you know that we must all be patient."

"Look what I found," chirped Rees. "A big jar and I've filled it with water from that spring. That's where the villagers must have got their water, see!" Cunval looked towards the clump of alder trees and nodded.

Glad of a drink and a short break, Cunval then went back to work. He had soon excavated into one corner of the building, and followed the wall around. He calculated that the dying had been laid against the walls and that nobody had the strength to move them later.

A bright green glint in the sunlight caught his eye. After he had cleared away the ashes and dust, a small copper cross appeared. It must have belonged to the priest. This was amazing luck.

The cross had been shielded somehow from the fire, or surely it would have melted. There was now just a chance that the amulet had also escaped the fire. With renewed vigour, he pulled at the stones, then, cleared the ash underneath. Whilst thinking about taking another rest and some water, he jerked bolt upright. Gold was gleaming in the dark corner near the back wall. He almost snatched at the amulet and held it up, shouting in triumph. It was gold, silver, and half-moon in shape. He had seen such things at the king's court in Caerleon. It was probably of Roman origin and it was so beautifully made. Cunval imagined that the old Yarl had been clutching it to him when he died, and it was completely undamaged.

When he rushed to the entrance of the enclosure, the children jumped up and down at Cunval's obvious delight. They all examined his find; the girls, especially, wanted to hold it to their necks.

"Rees, I think that you should carry this heirloom. After all, it belonged to your grandfather, and it may even be yours one day."

Cunval returned to the church, backfilled the rubble and left the heap rounded off. He reburied Dinabo's cross, with a special prayer and a whispered thank-you. Nature would soon clothe the bare stones with a green mantle.

The children told Cunval where all the houses and barns had been. They had found an iron axe-head, and this was to be a present for Catvael, with which to fight the Saxons. It was still some way off dusk and they had a long walk home, with Hawk, of course, leading the way.

After leaving the flat area of the old settlement, they approached a large, dead tree lying in the bank-side rushes. Hawk stopped and gave a low growl.

"I bet it's an otter," whispered Rees. "Let's have a look."

As they all moved forward, Hawk barked loudly. In the same instant, a terrifying masked figure jumped up and let out an angry shriek. The children scattered in fright and Cunval fell backwards in shock. The next thing he saw was a wolf's head, long braided plaits and foul-smelling fur close to his face. A spear was at his throat.

"It's Durwit!" shouted the terrified children.

Cunval desperately crawled backwards, making gasping sounds, when the truth dawned on him. This was Brockvael's shaman, and he was about to lunge with his spear. Cunval could see a pockmarked, greasy face under the wolf's head. Hawk was whining nearby, his tail between his legs, and the children shouted in unison, "Leave him alone."

"You filthy wretch," shouted the shaman. "I saw you desecrate my master's tomb. Nobody is to touch it. You die!"

"No, no, Brockvael sent us." Rees was tugging desperately at the shaman's arm.

The animal-like fiend eased himself backwards, shrugging off Rees' grip. Cunval tried to sit up, shaking like a leaf as the shaman glared at him with wild eyes.

"I'm Durwit, priest of Penhal," he growled. "You are a false priest, just like the last one. He brought the plague here and killed my master. You must leave Penhal, before you kill them too."

"Look Durwit, see what Cunval found in the church." Rees took the amulet from the safety of his pocket and Durwit howled like a banshee. He snatched the precious heirloom from Rees, and Cunval was powerless to wrest it from him.

"This belonged to my master. Any mortal touching it will die. I am the guardian!" Durwit leapt towards the river and plunged across the rapids, spray flew in all directions. In a moment, he was lost in the woods.

"Oh, no," cried Rees. "I should not have shown him the amulet. I was only trying to help you, Cunval. I thought he was going to spear you!"

"So did I, Rees. I've never been so frightened. I've not seen a pagan priest before." Cunval dusted down his tunic, breathing heavily.

"We've lost the amulet, now," Olwen was almost crying and the younger children were hanging on to her sleeves. "We must report to Brockvael, he will know where Durwit hides."

They all stayed closely together on the way home and avoided thick undergrowth. The little ones had started to wilt as they approached Penhal and made for the big hall.

As Cunval and Rees entered the hall, the younger children made for the side of the fire, where the women sat and worked. Brockvael was standing at the fireside and he turned to face them. They were amazed to see Brockvael hold up the amulet. Durwit must have run like the wind and given it to him.

Brockvael did not look happy. "Durwit tells me that

you tried to take the amulet from him."

"No, no, sire, I found it in the church, just as you asked." Cunval, breathless, was outraged at the shaman's lies.

Durwit emerged from the shadows, hissed at Cunval and shook a rattle in his face. "I found it first, master."

Rees tried to protest but, at that moment, the warriors, led by Catvael, barged into the hall, laughing and bragging. They cheered at the site of the amulet, as Brockvael swept away further talk and Cunval found himself jostled in the midst of the crowd.

"We must celebrate. Women, fetch the wine."

The old wife and the young wife went to the side of the hall where the drink was kept cool, and soon tankards were splashing wine, ale and cider onto the clay floor.

Catvael took Cunval's arm.

"We must be friends, young priest." Cunval judged that Catvael was about five years older than he was. "Here, have some cider. Now, let me see you drink this lot all in one go."

"I can't, sire." Cunval started to protest, but Catvael held the tankard firmly against his mouth. Cunval started to swallow. He was used to the occasional small mug of cider, which was full of the earth's goodness, but he knew that to drink a large tankard of cider would make him ill. After Cunval had spluttered through most of it, Catvael held out the tankard for re-filling, and all of the men howled with laughter as the priest's small frame was virtually held up in the air by Catvael. Cunval was aware of the smirking face of the sorcerer, Durwit, egging on the boisterous warriors who now surrounded him.

They took it in turns to examine the amulet and Catvael

then handed it to Cunval.

"Here, priest, come and show it to my woman."

Cunval was most surprised to be dragged through a hide curtain and into a partitioned room. He was aware of a figure moving towards the shutters and, as they opened, the low evening sunlight exploded through the window. As she turned towards the men, the long flaxen hair of a beautiful young woman drifted in the breeze. Her bearing and dignity left Cunval transfixed. His inebriating mind grasped the significance of her dress.

"You're a Saxon. You're so lovely." Cunval then addressed her in the Saxon language. He had known old Saxon slaves in Caerleon and had smuggled them food at night, so he had gained some knowledge of their strange tongue. The woman looked intently at Cunval but remained motionless.

Catvael swore at him and shook his arm fiercely.

"What did you say, you little worm? What did you say to my woman?"

"I'm sorry, sire. I only said good evening. I learnt some of the Saxon language in Caerleon, you see."

Cunval was thrown through the doorway, into Durwit, who had been lurking at the curtain. Picking himself up, Cunval stood his ground, swayed and then squared up to the shaman, who had shed his wolf's head, to reveal long greasy black hair.

"I'm not afraid of you, you disgusting pagan pig!"

The crowd fell silent for a moment and then burst out laughing. Cunval couldn't understand why he had said such a thing; he would never have had the courage normally. As he swayed forward, the shaman moved back apprehensively, then lunged at Cunval in temper and pushed him directly onto the fire. Brockvael was, by now, collapsed with laughter and started to cough and splutter uncontrollably. The women screamed and brushed the burning ashes from Cunval's tunic. At this point, the shaman dashed for the door and stormed off.

The next hour was a dream to Cunval. He was given bread and strong cheese and then plied further with wine. Eventually, he collapsed on the floor and crawled on hands and knees to the outside doorway. He was aware of Rees and his mother, Anhared, trying to hold him up, but he kept falling onto the muddy ground. Being sick on his tunic did not help his appearance.

They decided to take him to the river to wash, and as soon as they got to the slope, Cunval toppled and slid down the bank into the shallow water. His tunic was pulled off him and as Anhared dunked it and wrung it out, Rees helped him downstream to a pebbled beach. Cunval looked up to see a gathering crowd of the older people framed in the last of the sun's rays.

"Let us pray," he shouted, and started to sing out of tune. His undergarments were slipping as Henbut helped Rees to get Cunval up the bank and off to a safe bed.

chapter 9

The morning call startled Cunval. He had been having nightmares because of the unwelcome drinking bout and had dreamt that Catvael and Brockvael were pulling him into the river, with the children on the bridge laughing at him, whilst his two friends, the priests, Madoc and Tidiog, were on the bank, scolding him for dereliction of duty. As he gained consciousness and groaned at his aching head, Mair bathed his forehead with a cold cloth.

"You seem to have a fever, Father. You've been perspiring all night. The others have gone to the fields."

Cunval could not believe the hour; he had never slept so long in all his life. "The Saxon woman, I remember a Saxon woman with Catvael. What happened?"

"They got you drunk, Father, and I hear you saw Catvael's Saxon slave-girl. We all feel very sorry for her; she's only allowed out with Catvael himself. I fear you made an enemy of the shaman. He will try to trap you."

Cunval was sure of that. The previous day's events came back to him; it was so unjust. Durwit was going to be a difficult adversary. Cunval felt quite ill. He could only eat a small portion of bread, and he then insisted that his place was in the fields.

His tunic had once more been delivered to him dried out. He dare not ask how his undergarment had also been dried and placed at the foot of the bed. Determined though he was to tramp across the first field, he could not understand why he was perspiring so much.

Henbut and the labourers greeted him with a knowing smile.

"I'm sorry about last evening, gentlemen. I hope I did not embarrass you too much."

"Not at all, Cunval," teased Cam. "You do look a bit queer. I don't think you should be working today."

"I'll be all right. Honest work will cure me." An hour later, Cunval had collapsed and Cam, being the strongest, carried him back to Henbut's house.

"This man has a bad fever," declared Cam. "I don't think it's anything to do with the drink last night. Look how weak he is."

"I think you're right," Mair fussed over him. "I'll give him some medicines. Tell Henbut that I must report this to Brockvael's wife. It means that none of us will be allowed into the hall."

By the end of the day, panic had set in at the settlement. A fever could well turn into a plague. Nobody knew what to expect. It turned out that one of the old, retired workmen had gone down with a fever the previous evening, and although Henbut and Mair realised that Cunval could, therefore, not be the cause of the fever, Brockvael would not look at it this way. Cunval would get the blame; he had undoubtedly brought the fever from Caerleon.

By the evening, the Saxon woman and Brockvael's young wife had also succumbed, and they with others were put into make-shift beds in the hay barn. By the next day, the labourers were ill, and all the children were becoming feverish. They were put into their own house, with Anhared in charge. Brockvael and his older wife escaped infection and locked themselves inside the hall.

Catvael and his band had immediately decided to go to the farm through the forest, well to the west of the estate. They were due to make palisade defences because there were rumours of a Saxon raiding party, and this would a good chance to get away. As it happened, they escaped the fever.

Cunval was one of the first to recover, after a most uncomfortable three days. He had had fever before, and he knew how debilitating it was. He was thankful that it had not been a plague. He helped to care for the other sick people; running back and forth with broth and bread. Brockvael was greatly relieved at the gradual recovery, for he well remembered the disease that had finished off the old settlement. That plague, too, had supposedly been started by a priest. Durwit had made sure that the new priest carried the blame for the current fever.

Within a few days, however, things were getting back to normal, and calves and lambs were arriving. There was now an abundance of milk, and ploughing had recommenced. Cunval was not allowed into the hall, which suited him for the moment; in any case, he spent every moment he could at his enclosure. The children were quite excited by this building-up of a brand new home, and Rees, particularly, studied Cunval's every move.

Cunval was to be given a goat when he moved into his own hut; this would mean plenty of milk, and the goat would graze down the grass in his enclosure, at the same time providing manure for his garden. There was much to look forward to and, in some ways, after the scare of the fever, a closer tie with the people of the settlement had evolved.

The children were chirpy and mischievous again. Cunval was expected to resume his stories and keep them amused with the making of eel-traps and fish-traps. Among his possessions were an adze and a spoke-shave, carpentry tools that he put to good use by making benches, tables and beds. The children watched intently and had to try their hand, of course. He gradually introduced them to the wise words of Jesus and the disciples; the children enjoyed his enthusiastic efforts and always asked pertinent questions.

The old man who had first gone down with the fever had never recovered. His condition deteriorated and, a week later, he died. Cunval had visited regularly and, at the end, said prayers with Henbut and Mair. There could be no Christian burial. The shaman had been called, and Brockvael had arranged a pagan funeral in the normal way. Cunval, along with everybody else, was commanded to attend. He was very nervous, but realised he had to show respect. The thought of a pagan funeral was repugnant to him.

The following morning, a procession, led by Durwit, started from the old man's house and continued the short distance to the big pool. The warriors had returned from the west, and Cunval got the impression that they were a bit bored with the whole thing. The shaman wore a robe of white cattle skin and a feathered head-dress. His painted face could not disguise the fact that he revelled in the importance of his position. His rattle was annoying to Cunval, who started quietly humming to himself.

A dry-log funeral pyre had been built up on the river bank and, apart from Durwit's chanting, there was silence as the body was hoisted onto the pyre. Before long, flames had fiercely engulfed the whole mass. Durwit danced by the side of the big pool and the children looked on apprehensively. Some time went by, and, as the fire died down, Cunval and Henbut exchanged glances. Cunval reflected on the occasion. He could hardly blame these people for their beliefs; after all, it was his job to convert them from such an entrenched position. The labourers and the old people were simple and would follow any path on which their master led them. It was not going to be possible to convert Brockvael and it was doubtful whether his son, Catvael, would be anything other than hostile to the Christian concept.

Eventually, the fire died down enough for Durwit to use a long rake to drag all the remains down the bank and into the water. The fire had been so fierce that little remained of the human bones. The pool circled in a wide eddy and soon the whole surface was grey with ash.

Brockvael and the band of warriors returned to the hall for a drinking session, so Henbut offered to spend the rest of the day helping Cunval at his enclosure. The children, of course, wanted to help, and then they would go hunting with Hawk on the moor.

They all crossed the bridge, fooling around as usual, and had a race up the pathway. When Cunval reached the enclosure, his heart sank. His high wooden cross, which he had lovingly erected just inside the entrance, had been pushed down, and the few wattle panels that he had erected around his new garden had been smashed. The pool below the spring was filled with soil. Cunval sank to his knees. The children commiserated with him, and when Henbut arrived and surveyed the scene, the previous good mood had evaporated.

"Guess who!" said Henbut.

"You mean Durwit? Everything was fine yesterday. He must have done it in the night." Cunval felt humiliated.

"More likely, he came early this morning," replied Henbut. "The old priest told me, years ago, that Durwit is afraid of the dark and never goes out at night. He's probably afraid of his own imaginary gods and spirits."

Cunval knew that there was no-one to help him. Durwit could come at any time and do damage. Even when Cunval had built his hut, he could not always be there on his guard. Durwit could even burn the hut down while Cunval was away.

"Help us, Cunval!" Rees and the children were trying to push up the cross. The thongs binding the cross arm to the main shaft had been partly cut, so Cunval lashed it back together. He had made the cross from a straight length of dry oak that he had found in the wood, fashioned it with his adze and spoke-shave and polished it with sand and a flat stone.

"There. Now, we need to lift it back out of its hole first, then, I'll dig the hole out again, and make it deeper!"

This was soon done and the children held the cross upright while Cunval packed large stones around the base, in order to wedge the shaft firmly into the ground, and he then pummelled smaller stones into the spaces.

"Solid as a rock," declared Henbut, who had started digging the garden area. "Did you say you wanted some leaf-mould, Cunval?"

The children knew exactly why this was needed, and set

off into the adjoining woodland to gather the stickiest leaf-mould they could find. The digging and manuring went on expertly, and Rees used Cunval's pummel to help break up the virgin soil.

"There. You children can be off on the moor now. I'm sure you don't want to work all day." Cunval was grateful for any help, but he did not want the children to be bored. "I hope I'm not being too wicked, Henbut, but from what you say about Durwit, I think I might have a way to scare him off."

"Aha! You have a plan?"

"Well, sort of. Unless I stand up for myself, Durwit is going to try and drive me from here." Cunval was coming of age. His teaching over the last twelve years was all to do with dignity and resilience; any hardship had to be tackled head on.

"My turn for some digging, Henbut. Then we'll rest and I'll tell you the outline of my plan."

The rest of the day was well spent. Cunval cleared the pool, repaired and made more wattle fencing and started off the stone platform for his hut. That evening, the chatter in Henbut's house complemented Mair's excellent supper. A chicken had been killed, ready for the next day's supper, and the blood saved. Cunval had never eaten chicken, let alone saved chicken's blood; this gruesome task was yet another test of resolve.

Before dawn, Cunval prepared himself by the dim light of a lamp. His tunic was tied up, to expose his knobbly knees, and his sleeves were rolled up tightly, to show off his spindly arms. The next job, with chicken blood and Henbut's assistance, was to paint red spots and smears onto his arms, legs and face. Then, Cunval hastened off to the bridge and his enclosure. Dawn approached. Skirting the area of the enclosure, Cunval crawled into the hide in the bracken he had made the previous day. This gave a view of his garden and enclosure. He donned a ready-made head-dress of lamb's-tongue ferns and straw, and was glad that he could not see himself in this repulsive garb.

There was not long to wait. As the first of the sun's rays glided over the moor behind Cunval, he heard a noise in the woodland near the spring. Soon, Durwit crept out of the wood, half-naked, but with painted limbs. He surveyed the new work, looked into the clear pool, and then furiously drove his spear into the ground. From Durwit's demeanour, Cunval could sense that this was a man full of portent; he was, no doubt, imbued with all the spirits that he believed surrounded him. No doubt, Henbut was right; Durwit was probably afraid of the dark and could see dangerous ghosts in the guise of owls and night-jars.

Durwit pushed against the newly mounted cross; at this point Cunval's self-doubt disappeared. God worked in mysterious ways. As Durwit heaved with his shoulder, he heard a quiet cough behind him. Spinning around with a startled grunt, he confronted a weird apparition. Cunval staggered toward him, arms outstretched, groaning, "Plague! Plague!"

In one swift movement, Durwit fell backwards with a shriek, then bounded down the pathway. Cunval could hear him crashing through the woods below. Durwit was exposed.

The sense of relief was overpowering; Cunval sank to the ground below his cross shouting, "Thank you, thank you, Lord."

Almost immediately, a sense of guilt came over him; had he done the right thing? It was too late now; there was only one thing for it. Grabbing Durwit's spear, Cunval raced through the higher level of the woods, and parallel to the river. Somewhere, Durwit had a hideaway. There must be a lair that he retreated to at night.

The path that Cunval followed allowed him to travel swiftly and silently. He knew that the big pool was now somewhere down below him, so he stopped and listened. Despite his heavy breathing, he detected the crack of a twig breaking underfoot, somewhere downhill. Continuing along the same route for almost a mile, Cunval caught an occasional glimpse of a figure striding along a lower pathway. Durwit was tiring, but he was making for a definite spot.

Cautiously, Cunval crept through the woodland, which was now in bright daylight. He wondered for a moment if he had lost his quarry; had he gone to ground? Hiding behind a fallen log, Cunval waited awhile, listening. There was much noise from the woodland birds; then a chattering blackbird gave the game away. Somebody was in a large blackthorn thicket. As Cunval peered with narrowed eyes, an ivy-clad screen moved to one side and Durwit appeared, completely oblivious of any other presence. He clutched a leg of pig-meat, and gnawed on it furiously. He was clearly very annoyed and presently threw the bone down the bank towards the river. Sitting down, with his head in his hands, Durwit looked a pathetic figure.

After a while, some noisy ducks on the river-bank caused Durwit to look up. He closed the screen to his lair and ran off down the hill; this was Cunval's chance. Being sure that

Durwit was by now far away, Cunval crept down to the thicket and pulled at the screen. The smell was nauseating; the lair had been dug into the bank, underneath an outcrop of rock, to form a cave, and a wretched collection of pagan junk made Cunval wince. There were bones, feathers, sticks, stones, jars and hides. It was no wonder that Durwit was consumed by his own bogies and spirits.

Cunval staggered into the fresh morning air and closed the screen. He still had Durwit's spear in his hand; he knew not why, he would never want to use it. Snapping the shaft of the spear across his knee, he threw it down. When Durwit saw it, he would know that Cunval's magic was as good as his own was.

chapter 10

As he made for the bridge downstream, Cunval was aware of the chicken blood still painted on his body. He was near the big pool; now, he decided, that would be just the place to wash. He made for a sandy patch where the water was shallow and waded in up to this knees. As he washed he said a prayer for the old man whose funeral the day before he had resented.

Smugness was a sin, but was it not ironic that he should be standing in Durwit's sacred pool on such a satisfactory occasion? He knew that he must now be on guard because Durwit would be plotting. Cunval washed himself vigorously.

Mair had saved him some eggs, and the morning meal fortified him for what would be a pleasurable day's ploughing and hoeing. He would not relate the story of Durwit's humiliation, but Henbut would know from his demeanour that all had gone smoothly.

The April days slipped by. Soon it was Eastertide, and Cunval held brief services with Henbut and Mair at the high Cross. His thoughts were sometimes with his brethren at Caerleon. He was not homesick, which surprised him; there was far too much to do. He felt that if he was still intact and living as a member of the community, then he had achieved his first goal, but there was so much still to do, and Cunval constantly fretted. He must not falter, especially as Durwit would be spreading lies at every opportunity.

Cunval was very grateful for the assistance of Rees. As Brockvael's favourite, Rees was able to explain that Cunval was not responsible for bringing storms, for the loss of a calf, or lamb, or whatever mishap for which he usually got the blame. Cunval reflected on Brockvael's father, whose bones had been left at the old settlement. If he had died in the church, then surely he had been converted by the old priest, Dinabo. Perhaps, Brockvael knew this and was afraid of the new religion.

Rees was old enough to please himself where he went and, although he was the leader of the children, sometimes he enjoyed being alone with Cunval. Some evenings, as it grew lighter, he joined Cunval at the enclosure. The garden area had been safely enclosed against animals, and wheat and field beans had been planted, using seed from the communal store. Cunval's own seeds he would plant when his hut was built. The hut was now the priority, and Rees wanted to be there at every stage. Cunval was a very average carpenter, but Rees was learning well and he loved to stand back and gaze when each job was completed. All the children helped with the gathering of rushes for the thatch.

The ploughing of the main fields continued until the end of April, and soon the seeds were sown. There were several types of cereals, but the field beans covered a huge area; they were the mainstay in the winter months.

The first of May arrived, when there was to be a festival called Beltane, involving the blessing of the crops and the celebration of the high summer. Thankfully, Cunval was not obliged to go to the revered pagan spring near the settlement. Henbut and Mair were always absent from these ceremonies, because they were Christians, and one of Durwit's duties was to sacrifice a lamb and smear the blood over his body. Durwit's position was still unassailable, and he avoided contact with Cunval, which was pleasing.

The day arrived when Cunval was due to move to his new hut.

The base timber and the main timbers were of oak, the walls of wattle and clay daub. The thatched roof was lofty and he could easily stand up indoors. A floor of flat stones was to remain uncovered, and at the west end was his bed. In the centre was a raised area for his small fire, and the important east end, for the moment, was bare. This was to be the position for his altar that he was now hacking from a thick slab of stone. The altar would have a small cross carved at each corner and would be the focal point for his meagre possessions: two candles, and an old Roman decorated bowl for use as a chalice. He would carve a small altar cross from yew wood, all to be highly polished and waxed. The first night in his new home would feel strange, but fulfilling.

Cunval now had his own goat. With the entrance to his enclosure screened off, the goat was confined inside, and soon the grass was cropped short and most pleasing to the eye. Cunval dug out any unsightly dock plants, and fussed around his garden, watering each row. With a made-up length of rope tied to a log as a tether, Cunval was able to take the goat onto the moor to graze. The cattle were frequent visitors and enjoyed rubbing their necks against his fencing. Naturally, Cunval had to fit extra posts and braces. Still, cattle were pleasant to talk to and they much appreciated some ivy and freshly leafed branches that he pulled down for them. They were especially fond of young oak leaves.

Towards the end of May, a strange thing happened. Cunval was helping Rees to make a new bench, as a present for his mother. Rees was doing most of the work, and the bench was to be low and sturdy and to stand beside the hearth in the hall.

They looked up to see Catvael and the Saxon woman watching them. They had obviously been walking on the moor, and Cunval thought how happy they looked together. The Saxon woman, as before, looked very attractive, and this caused Cunval to look away.

"Rees is a good boy." The Saxon woman spoke to Cunval in her own language.

"Yes," said Cunval, automatically replying in the Saxon tongue. "He will be a good carpenter." Cunval roughed Rees' hair and the woman laughed. Catvael looked uneasy.

"My name is Helga. What is that wood?" she pointed to the cross. "Does it keep away evil spirits?"

Cunval stood up and stroked the cross lovingly; he realised that Helga's religion was no better than that of the Celtic pagans; the Saxons were known to offer human sacrifices after battles. He was thinking of a suitable reply, when Catvael took her arm and they hurried off. Rees looked at Cunval and pulled a face.

The weather was now warm and the heavy farming work was complete. There was one more task to do in the community garden before the next rain: the preparation of the tilth.

"We've hammered this poor soil until it's like sand," complained Cam. "If this is to be a luxury garden, I think

I'll stick to beans." The whole clan was interested in the well-fenced garden area just outside the rear palisade. Food was a high priority on any estate, and the thought of new types of food was most interesting. The people now looked up to Cunval and respected his modern knowledge.

Cunval, as usual, was meticulous; the fine tilth of the garden was divided by pathways, every measurement double checked. Even the warriors and Brockvael had taken an interest in this elaborate geometry; measurements and scales had left this region with the Romans long ago.

Henbut and the labourers willingly took Cunval's orders for the planting of the seeds. The special onions were interspersed with the carrots, turnips and beet, and the celery and peas had their own spacious sections. Plum and cherry seeds were spaced in their own raised bed, for later transplanting to the orchard, and the whole area was lightly covered with latticed panels to keep off the birds. Cunval had shown the labourers how to burn limestone, which he now needed to spread near the seedbeds as a protection against slugs, a good quantity of lime having been dug in with the manure.

Slowly, spring moved into summer and the farming chores became lighter. Cunval spent more time with the older folk and encouraged the children to help them with their daily chores and with their routine of light work.

Brockvael summoned Cunval to the Hall. This usually meant a complaint, so Cunval could hardly disguise his delight when Brockvael also called in Rees and spoke.

"I want you to take Rees to Abermenei, stay there three days and then bring me back some wine. Pedur will have it for me from the King."

Cunval's heart jumped; this would mean a visit to brother Tidiog. He knew that barges came up the Gwei with goods and returned with wheat and timber. He also knew from Henbut that Rees was of an age where he would now be introduced to the people of Abermenei. As a nobleman's grandson, Rees would meet the other children of his age and they would become lifelong friends and, later, comrades-in-arms. The tribal bond was strong throughout the land.

"Yes, sire," stuttered Cunval. "He will be safe with me, of course. When do we leave?"

"Now!"

Rees whooped and asked his mother for food for the journey. Cunval looked down at his dilapidated sandals. His feet were considerably toughened and he often went barefoot.

It was mid-morning when they left, and Hawk whined loudly at being left behind. However, they were taking with them a young bitch, as a present for Pedur. She was as excited as Rees and ran in circles around the first few fields. Cunval carried his sandals tied onto his belt; he would need them in the town.

The walk was longer than Cunval had remembered, but there was a sense of freedom, now that they were away from the settlement, and Rees could feel it too. They saw the new summer wildlife. Families of ducks and moorhens seemed to be everywhere on the water, fish were snapping at flies on the surface, and dragonflies and midges danced in the sunlight.

An occasional salmon jumped in the deeper pools, and Rees pointed excitedly. This explosion of life was central to the Celtic notion of birth, life and death.

Rees seemed to be reading his thoughts. "If your God creates all the new animals and birds, does he create human babies too? And what about Saxon babies? Surely, he doesn't create them?"

"He does indeed. You see, life is a sort of test. As you grow up and become wiser, then you know that hurting or killing is wrong and, so, the wiser you become the more you can reject bad things."

"You said that we must not hate other people. Who is going to say that to the Saxons? I bet that you wouldn't try to tell them." Rees pulled a face.

"Yes, it is difficult. I have to be honest with you, Rees. I just don't know at present. Perhaps, one day, Helga may discover our God and then she can tell them. I know that she's a good person." Cunval realised that he had said "our" God.

Rees sighed and plodded on. It was going to be hard to grow up and be faced with having to think all the time.

They eventually arrived at the confluence of the Menei and Gwei. Rees let out a whistle at this wonder.

"Just look at the size of that river! I came here with Pa once, when I was little, but I don't remember much. It's huge. I bet it's full of big salmon.

"Did you remember your father, Rees?"

The subject had never cropped up before. His father, Maelwyn, had been killed in a battle with the Saxons, far to the east. An army led by the king had joined with other armies from other tribes to push the Saxons back to the eastern sea, and many had died on both sides.

"Only that he used to pick me up a lot and bite my neck. Olwen doesn't remember him. Ma and Grandfather were upset. And Uncle Catvael was a only a young man then."

"I'm so sorry, Rees. Life just isn't fair sometimes."

Cunval shuddered to think of the dismay of the clan on hearing the news of the loss. This had occurred six years earlier and now, once more, there had been rumours that the Saxons were pushing west again in small war parties. Cunval could not understand why they would want to kill, burn and loot. Surely, there was enough land for everybody to share.

"I meant to tell you, Rees. When I was young, I lived near the sea, beyond Caer Taf, and one night, some Scotti pirates raided us. Many of our own warriors were killed and we all fled. When we got back, my older sister was missing, and another girl. They had been taken as slaves, you know. I pray for them every day."

Rees grunted, he didn't know what to say, but it was another bond between them. Cunval suddenly realised that, in some way, he was probably replacing Rees' father. He patted him on the shoulder as they moved on to the town.

chapter 11

The children of the town had seen the visitors approaching in the dusk, and had run out to greet them. The young bitch had been keenly trotting in front of Cunval and Rees all the way down-river, and she now ran towards the children, whining and rolling over in the grass. Perhaps she knew that she was at her new home. Rees was a bit embarrassed to have such a large gang charging up and staring at him; an older boy in the group of town children looked rather aggressive, which Cunval had half expected, with his long experience of teaching young lads. As leader, the boy was wary of any threat from outside.

"Now then, children, I'd like you to meet Rees. He's the grandson of Yarl Brockvael. We've come to stay for a few days." Cunval took the older boy by the shoulder. "Now, you seem to be the boss around here. What's your name?"

"Conmael," the boy stated gruffly.

"Right. Shake hands, then. Now, Conmael, can you introduce all your friends, please."

They all shook hands in turn, keeping a fixed stare at the newcomer. Cunval moved off, Conmael close at his heels.

"As you probably know already, we have come to report to Pedur. Rees will be staying with him. I know, Conmael, why don't you run on with Rees to Pedur's house, and tomorrow you can show him around the town, and let him see the weir and the fishing nets?"

"Come on then, Rees," called Conmael, setting off at speed. The other children all watched as the two boys began to race across the field.

"I bet Conmael wins," said one of the boys.

"He's very fast," agreed Cunval. "Now, who's going to tell me all the latest news? Is Tidiog well?"

"Yes," offered one of the girls. "He buried my great-grandmother in his cemetery last week. She was a Christian, you know. All the family watched."

This was pleasing; it showed that Christianity had at least been accepted in this area without too much prejudice.

"I expect you loved her very much," said Cunval. "She will be in heaven now."

The girl shrugged her shoulders. "She used to live at the old settlement before the plague, and she was related to Yarl Brockvael's family, but she lost her mind in the end."

Walking along the river bank towards the town, they exchanged other news. The king's messengers, it seemed, had been coming back from the east and passing quickly through.

Pedur and his wife looked genuinely pleased to see Cunval. Rees and Conmael were already at the house, drinking hot milk and laughing together. They were going to explore the river early in the morning. The fishing nets were of great interest to Rees, and his new friend was going to explain everything to him.

Cunval was obliged to stay for supper, and reported to Pedur, in the minutest detail, all the news of Penhal. Rees commanded the floor, telling of the expedition to find the amulet, and he was not afraid to expose Durwit's devious plot.

"I will not have even a soothsayer in my town," said Pedur. "I don't trust any of them."

When Pedur had started to slur after a few goblets of wine, Cunval took his leave, to spend the night with Tidiog.

Tidiog was delighted when he heard Cunval's shout from the darkness. They hugged each other affectionately and exchanged news.

"There! I told you everything would work out. You look so healthy. Now, have you converted Brockvael yet?"

The light from Tidiog's small lamp and the glowing fire reflected warmly off the newly lime-washed walls.

"No. I think it will be another twenty years before that happens. I can't complain though; he tolerates me, and that's all I ask." Cunval was enthusiastic in his story of the Penhal mission, and clapped his hands with joy at each turn of events, especially the exposure of Durwit.

"I hear you had a recent burial, Tidiog."

"Yes, and the funny thing was, another elderly person died a few weeks ago. It was an old labourer, and he was buried in the old Roman cemetery that I showed you. Anyway, his wife asked me to attend and say a few prayers. So there you are; people are starting to think."

Cunval slept well after the long day's walk. With no urgent business, Cunval spent the next three days helping Tidiog. The two priests were familiar with Roman masonry, and they built up and repaired one of the burnt-out ruins for Pedur. This was to be a stable and store. The children watched and, of course, took part until it got boring. They tried to build their own hut and, with the help of the priests, a small house and its own garden rose from the rubble. The planting of seeds was shared by all the children, and fencing was erected, to keep out the older folk.

Rees and Conmael got along fine; they would both be trained as warriors one day. The new bitch had bonded with the children, and arrangements were made for Conmael and the older children to visit Penhal later in the summer.

The three days had passed quickly and, after a last breakfast with Tidiog, Cunval was called to the storehouse to collect Brockvael's wine. He lifted the wine amphora and gasped.

"It's so heavy, Pedur. I'll never carry this all the way to Penhal. It will take me two days."

Pedur laughed. "You've got to take two, Cunval. They travelled up-river from the king, only last month, and they're all the way from the Mediterranean. Brockvael will go mad if there's any damage."

Cunval was in despair at this impossible task.

"There's also something else for you to take." Pedur and Rees grinned and Cunval winced. "Here, in the new stable, is a donkey for Penhal."

Cunval heaved a sigh of relief; Pedur had certainly had his fun. He called in one of his men to harness the animal and fix the two amphorae securely. Cunval's natural curiosity incited him to help; he took careful note of the style of harnessing required.

"Thank Brockvael for the dog. She's going to be a beauty. He will mate the donkey as he sees fit and it can be returned another time."

The whole gang set off to escort Cunval and Rees for the first half-mile. Tidiog joined them as the children played on the riverbank and tumbled in the long grass, and at midmorning, they said their farewells.

Cunval was delighted with the donkey; he would use him to transport the winter's firewood to the settlement. He was going to be worth his weight in gold.

The trip was uneventful and they arrived home well before dark. The wine was carefully unloaded; one amphora was stored away and the other was hung in a cradle from the rafters, for immediate use. Brockvael was in jovial mood and Cunval dared to ask if he and Rees could take charge of the donkey and introduce him to the clan's female donkey. Then they could use them both for collecting firewood.

Brockvael waved his arm, which seemed to mean approval, and Cunval retired to Henbut's house, to give them all the news of Abermenei. Rees led the donkey to meet his new mate.

Judging from the noise that emanated from their paddock during the night, Cunval knew that the two donkeys were happy with each other. The next few days were spent collecting firewood. All the children were expected to help; an enormous quantity was needed before the next winter. Selected trees in the surrounding woods had been felled, two winters ago, and allowed to dry. Roots were also grubbed up; they would keep the fires smouldering all night when it was frosty.

The labourers had large axes and, first, they set about the long trunks. Cunval and Rees chopped the smaller branches, and the children helped, in between playing games. Much timber was gathered from the riverbanks, where the winter floods had kindly deposited it. Most of this was already dry, and the smaller driftwood was tied tightly in bundles.

These were pleasant days. The crops were growing nicely

and the rainstorms seemed to come at just the right time. The whole settlement was happy. Cunval was elated when, one Sunday evening, Henbut and Mair came, as usual, to his service and brought with them an elderly, gentle couple who had appreciated Cunval's help during the fever. They had to be helped up the hillside, and Cunval quickly made up a bench for them to sit on. They had not been on the hillside for some years and were amazed at Cunval's enclosure and his fussy garden. Cunval had donned his hooded cape for the occasion, and his copper cross, nicely polished, was hanging over his tunic.

The new couple found the large wooden cross, where Cunval stood, very imposing. His prayers in Latin were an incomprehensible mystery, as usual, so he quickly moved on to the parables and the wise counsel of the disciples. Everybody nodded their approval and, after milk and honey with cake, it was time to return home. It was doubtful whether the elderly couple would ever manage to come again to Cunval's enclosure, so he arranged for further services at Henbut's house, if it suited all concerned.

Rees was now spending time with the warriors, when they were home, being taught archery, riding, wrestling and stalking of the enemy. Cunval knew that he dared not interfere. A grand tournament was arranged, for the warriors to show off their prowess, and Cunval gasped when Durwit, who was the adjudicator, appeared in his full battle-dress. The tournament was held in the large field by the big pool, and the whole settlement attended.

The children grew excited when Durwit gave a signal with his rattle, and all eyes looked up the hill. The warriors made a breathtaking entrance over the brow of the hill, nine horsemen giving blood-curdling yells, spears high in the air. They charged around the field, followed by the hound dogs, and threw their spears at dummy enemy soldiers suitably lined up along the riverbank. Cunval realised that, with each thud of a spear, an enemy soldier would be killed instantly. He shivered and thought of his own brother, who he well knew had fought in real battles.

The children were then picked up by the riders, and taken for a gentler ride around the field. The younger ones looked scared at first, but jumped for joy when returned to the ground. Bows were then unstrapped from the backs of the warriors, and the dishevelled dummies jerked with each arrow that cut into them. Brockvael explained to the crowd that the most important and the most difficult manoeuvre was about to come.

Durwit's rattle together with his odious cursing set the scene. The warriors did a tight circuit, charging past the crowd and towards the dummies. They went past them for a little way, swivelled in their horned saddles, and fired arrows behind them with great accuracy at the targets. The children gasped loudly.

It was obvious that Catvael was not only the leader, but also the strongest and most skilful warrior. His right-hand man, Arteg, was next in line, and the others made up a formidable team. Cunval tried not to think of war; but he knew that evil people had to be countered somehow.

When the warriors rode back down the hill, they formed a line and stopped opposite the dummies. The horses kneeled and then lay down as the bows were drawn. The dogs barked fiercely every time they saw the bows, and snapped furiously as the warriors, facing uphill, fired arrow after arrow at an imaginary enemy charge. Then, with a blood-curdling cry, they turned about, drew their swords, and charged the dummies. With the slashing and thrusting, the dummies quickly fell to pieces under the onslaught. With loud cheers of triumph from Durwit and the crowd, the warriors waved their swords in the air. This type of warfare was a direct legacy from Roman times.

However, all was not over; four of the warriors fell and feigned injury. Their comrades picked them up and hoisted them over their shoulders, running at the same time to the waiting horses. With the wounded safely across the saddles, they all galloped up the hill.

This was a most impressive display and Brockvael waved his arms violently and dared any enemy to come near his clan. When Durwit strode to the pool and started howling a silly chant, Cunval slipped away.

Chapter 12

Well up-river, beyond the old settlement at Hentland, stood Blaeno, one of the outlying farmsteads, which also served as a watch-place for the northern district. Two of Catvael's warriors came from this place, leaving their families to farm the land. A young man named Maervun, from Blaeno, had reported to Penhal for military training, for he was now sixteen and eager to join the war band. He was the brother of one of the experienced warriors, and had brought with him a fine horse.

Cunval was once more summoned to Brockvael.

"I have just received a message from my great aunt, Freid. I don't understand why, but she's always been a Christian. She says that she's dying and wants the new priest to visit her at Blaeno. That's you." Cunval nodded gravely. "You can leave at first light and stay there until she dies."

Cunval sensed that Brockvael was using this opportunity to get rid of him. Probably, he was worried about Cunval's increasing popularity, especially with the children. Still, this might be a good thing in some ways; the warriors were uneasy with Cunval's presence, and had consolidated their own worship of Mars, the Roman god of war, almost as if they were hoping for war.

Meeting Fried would provide a welcome break for Cunval, who was pleased to know that a Christian survived at the Blaeno farmstead. Cunval had not dared to ask for permission to visit other farms while there was work to do at Penhal. Henbut was happy for him to go now, and Mair prepared food for the journey. He was also to deliver spare seed corn and rough salt, of which the Blaeno people would be glad. His backpack would be put to good use once more.

Rees was disappointed to be left out, but promised to visit Cunval's hut and tend the goat and the garden during his absence. Cunval took the precaution of hiding his meagre possessions, just in case Durwit decided to take advantage of the situation. He packed his candles and chalice, but decided to leave his heavy cloak behind.

The trip to Hentland was uneventful, and Cunval rested and ate a light meal with milk. He lingered at the old church ruins and said prayers before setting off again up the beautiful river valley. He felt comfortable surrounded by nature; he felt that God's handiwork was most excellent.

The few survivors of the plague at Hentland had been sent up to the farmstead at Blaeno. They had not been allowed to move until the plague was fully abated, and Brockvael had forbidden any to go to Penhal. Brockvael's great aunt must have known Dinabo, the old priest, intimately and Cunval hoped that she was going to be well enough to describe the old times at the settlement.

Blaeno was placed in an ideal setting, on a south-facing slope, high above the river. The crops in the surrounding fields looked healthy, and the farm animals and their offspring were lying contentedly in the evening sunlight. A small group of children were, as usual, the first to charge out to meet him. Their greeting was genuinely warm, and Cunval wondered whether the elderly lady had pre-empted his Bible stories and had told them of Jesus. Firstly, he must report to the overseer in the stockade, and this turned out to be a pleasant surprise. Cunval had expected hostility after the events at the old settlement, but he was treated like a long lost friend. The old priest had done good work before his unfortunate demise.

The overseer, Mark, was a jovial man in his fifties and was no great friend of Brockvael. His own son had been killed in the same battle as Rees' father, and his life was now devoted to the farm. After refreshment in the hall, they went to see the old lady in her home near by.

"I'm so glad to meet you, Cunval. I know all about you. Word travels, you know." Cunval was surprised to see an elderly, dignified lady standing upright by the fire and leaning on a stick. Her slightly younger companion sat at a table.

"I thought that you might not be well," said Cunval, masking his perplexity with some difficulty. "I had a message that you were quite ill."

"You may not think so, but I am, in fact, dying. I've asked you here to grant my last wish. I want to spend my few remaining days at Penhal. Brockvael would not approve, if he knew of my plan beforehand. He hates Christians. Sit down, both of you."

Cunval looked sideways at a smirking Mark.

"It's not for me to argue," explained Mark with a shrug. "This old woman has a will of iron."

"I'm glad to see you so fit, my lady. I have to say, there's a wonderful atmosphere here at Blaeno. I feel you have blessed this place."

"I dare say, Cunval. In a way, I have carried on the work of dear Dinabo. Mark and his family are good people, and you must spend some time here before we set off. And, Father Cunval, do call me Freid."

"Set off? Can you travel, my lady? It is rough going, on the back of a horse."

"No, travel on horseback would finish me off, but we have a canoe. I shall enjoy the journey downriver. Are you experienced with a canoe and paddle?"

"No. I've never canoed on a river before."

Mark interrupted. "I'll teach you, Cunval. You needn't worry. You can swim, can't you?"

"No! I'm afraid of deep water." This was not what Cunval had expected at all; it did not sound very safe, and Brockvael would, no doubt, be happy to drown him.

Mark could hardly conceal his mirth. "Freid," he asked, "will you join us for supper tonight? We have some very tender venison, and all the families will be sharing our table."

"Cunval can't eat meat, I understand. Make sure that he has some of my smoked trout, and give him some of the preserved plums." Freid turned to Cunval as Mark took his leave. "You may be wondering how I know so much about you. My very good companion here, Elma, has been to see Brockvael's wife. We keep in touch. She's a dear friend of mine." Cunval nodded to Elma and smiled. "One reason for me wanting to go to Penhal is to see her again," Fried continued, "and all the family, of course. I want to give her my jewellery, which won't be of any use to me soon."

Cunval felt there was no point in discussing the journey any further; Freid was going to get her way, whatever happened. He changed the subject.

"You remember young Rees, of course, Brockvael's grandson. He's going to be a fine lad. He's always willing to help, and he learns so quickly. I wonder if you will recognise him now."

"Good. I haven't seen him since he was a child, or Olwen. I'm so looking forward to seeing them all. Catvael calls occasionally and brings me presents. He's so headstrong, I fear he will get himself into trouble one day. He will never accept Christianity, you know."

Freid poked at the fire with her stick. "Now, I expect you will want me to tell you all about the old days at Hentland. I must see the old place again, just once, to say goodbye to everybody. Brockvael's father was just converted, you know, when the plague struck. He was such a good man, always fair."

They talked until suppertime, and then talked again into the night. Cunval learned so much from Freid and felt humbled in her presence. It appeared that Durwit avoided Blaeno, using Christianity and the plague as an excuse. Cunval felt safe in relating his own experience of Durwit, which caused great amusement, and they both agreed that he was dangerous, but a fraud. The next morning saw the priest's initiation into water transport. Cunval changed into suitable clothes, and was given water wings made from sheep's intestines. The children had been playing in the dugout canoe, making the whole exercise look easy. Mark then explained the intricacies of balancing, back-paddling, and beaching. However, the first exercise -getting into the canoe -had not been explained, and Cunval immediately tipped over and caught his face on the gravel bottom. Standing knee-deep in the water and trying to stem the flow of blood from his nose was not what he had expected. He had to lie on the bank for a while to recover.

The depth of water in the Menei was usually no more than chest-high, but the deep pool where they practised did not help Cunval's phobia, especially as the children rescued him after each capsize, recovering the canoe and baling it out. After a full day, he was able to paddle up and down the river well enough and quite enjoyed the experience. The children at Penhal would be proud of him. He had usually found work to do when they were on the deeper parts of the river.

Mark took pride in showing Cunval all over the homestead and was surprised at Cunval's knowledge of farming. They soon forged a close friendship and Cunval felt that Mark found Christianity quite acceptable. There were no pagan shrines at Blaeno, as Fried had been able to discourage them; the seeds were sown. When Cunval started to tell the children stories, the rest of the community listened in. Cunval was now an old hand at story-telling and could embellish the facts to suit the mood. The children, as usual, wanted the gruesome details.

The farm labourers were respectful towards Cunval. He was able to pass on messages from the workers at Penhal, and promised to give all the Blaeno news in return. It was only once a year, after harvest, that the labourers could visit their colleagues and relatives at other farms. They were then allowed to make merry, which usually involved much ale-drinking and the secret insulting of the idle warriors.

The morning start to the down-river trip involved practice runs with Fried in the canoe; she came aboard without difficulty. A board had been set up by Cunval, which allowed Fried to sit upright in the front of the canoe, facing him, with her few belongings stored behind her in the bow. She was also equipped with buoyancy bags -just in case.

"That's enough, Cunval. Let's be off now." Fried, satisfied that she would eventually get to Penhal, did not want to linger with tears in her eyes. A wave of her stick was her last goodbye to Blaeno.

Cunval struggled to keep the canoe in the centre of each set of rapids. Sometimes there was an ominous scraping of the bottom in shallower water, but they made it in good time to the old settlement.

"Pull in by here, Cunval." Freid pointed with her stick. "This will be the easiest way for me to get to the church. I remember it all so well." Cunval was able to help her safely out of the canoe and, with his supporting arm, they made for the church ruin.

"I imagine you found the amulet near that corner." Again Freid pointed her stick.

"Why, yes," replied Cunval. "How did you know?"

"That's where he died; the dead were all placed around the walls and left there. We had no strength to do otherwise, but, at least, the church was consecrated. The children died first. They are all near the altar. I do hope this place is never disturbed, Cunval."

"Shall we have a burial service? I'm sure it will be all right, even after all this time."

"Good idea, but not in that Roman language. I never did understand that."

Cunval quietly carried out his service.

They were soon back on the river, and Freid congratulated Cunval on his avoidance of any mishaps. Cunval had been concentrating so much on his duty that they were almost onto the big pool before he realised and remembered the rules.

"Oh, no! I almost forgot. I'm not allowed onto the sacred pool with the canoe. We'll have to land somewhere, and then I must somehow drag the canoe past the pool. I'll have to assist you along the bank."

"Nonsense! I've been on this river all my life. I'll deal with Durwit and that damn fool Brockvael. Paddle on."

"I can't. I must obey the rules of the Yarl. It's my duty."

Cunval started to steer for the beach, at which point Freid grabbed his paddle and held it behind her. The canoe started to drift sideways and then glided down the rapids into the centre of the pool. Cunval was about to bury his head in his hands with despair when there was a bloodcurdling cry from the wooded, far bank. Cunval was surprised to see two people. Durwit and a boy of about fifteen stood screaming abuse at them. They had obviously been following the canoe down-river for some time. This was going to mean big trouble. Durwit and his companion ran down the bank, howling. Brockvael was going to be utterly livid. Freid handed back the paddle and Cunval made furiously for the exit rapids; he was in time to see Durwit racing across the bridge to the hall.

"Over there," said Freid calmly. "That's a good place for me to land."

"Who was that boy, Freid? I've never seen him before," Cunval was quite shocked to think that Durwit was extending his obnoxious influence to youngsters.

"That's young Durwas. He's Durwit's nephew; an evil little devil if ever there was one. Of course, you wouldn't know of Durwit's father, the old pagan priest. His name was Mortal, and the family lived up in the hills to the north. The less you know of those days, the better!"

The canoe settled on the shingle. The events that followed were predictable. The whole band of warriors had come rushing to the river-bank in response to Durwit's cacophony, and, having sized up the situation, they dragged Cunval up the bank and threw him to the ground. Freid's protestations were ignored and she was led away to the hall.

Chapter 13

"You dare to insult our gods," shouted Catvael into Cunval's ear. Everything was a blur as Cunval felt himself being dragged along by many hands. His head was now underwater and he gasped for breath. The angry noise had subsided, but fingernails were digging into his soft flesh. When his head was finally jerked upwards, he found himself staring down into the sacred well, and he thought he was going to be drowned.

"This well is dedicated to our god Maponus, and you are going to pay homage to him. You dared to touch our sacred pool and now you will pay with your life. Pray if you can. See if your god will help you!"

Cunval's head was once more thrust into the well. As he choked on the ice-cold water, he prayed. Maponus could have his flesh but he would never submit his spirit. Cunval did not struggle and, nearing unconsciousness, he was once more pulled upright. The shouting continued and, as his eyes cleared, he looked skywards. There was even worse horror to behold; shrivelled and grotesque animal heads were hanging down from the roof of the shrine in which he was held. Statuettes and ribbons and feathers, like the ones in Durwit's filthy lair, lined the stone walls. This odious den of hell was too much for Cunval; with strength that shocked his captors, he broke free, stumbled from the shrine and ran for the river. He tumbled into the water and was trapped by the mud and weeds.

"Don't kill him, Catvael." Cunval looked up to see Arteg holding Catvael's arm, which was braced with a spear. "Think of the king." Catvael's temper subsided and there was no doubt that Cunval had been within an inch of his life.

Catvael stormed off, with his warriors in tow. A crowd had gathered on the bank and they stared down at Cunval with horror. The women whisked the crying children into the hall.

Henbut and Rees motioned for a badly bruised Cunval to wade to the shingle beach, and they then helped him towards the bridge.

"I think you should go to your hut," whispered Henbut. "You should never have gone onto the pool. They were going to kill you, you know."

Cunval knew that he could not blame Freid, probably the women would soon know the truth. For the moment, he must get to his hut, pray and think. He had been prohibited from entering the shrine in the past, and he would certainly never enter it again. To think that, all this time, he had been drinking the water collected from that heathen well. Inside his hut and with the door half closed, Cunval noticed that his small fire was ready for lighting. Rees had left everything in order and, obviously, Durwit had kept clear.

Now, however, Cunval must fully expect to have his hut burnt down and the enclosure destroyed. No matter, he must stay at this spot and persevere, whatever the difficulties. He would have to hide all his possessions; he could not afford to lose his precious chattels. What would

Bishop Dyfrig advise? Should he stay put, or should he go immediately to Brockvael and try to apologise for breaking the law? His goat tenderly pushed her head through the doorway, as if to offer sympathy, and the birds sang softly in the evening light. At least, he was not alone.

Wringing out his clothes and hanging them up to dry, he donned a spare, thin tunic that he sometimes used for working. Cunval crawled gratefully into his bed; he had not meant to fall asleep, but the day's exertions took their toll. Unpleasant dreams filled Cunval's head. He could clearly see evil imps and water sprites in the well, grabbing at his hair; he could smell the shrunken animal heads. He could, somehow, see the heads of Saxons killed in battle, with Catvael cheerfully decapitating wounded warriors on the battlefield.

A shout caused Cunval to jump from his bed. It was dusk.

"Don't let me disturb you, Cunval." It was Cam, the labourer.

Cunval wrapped himself in his cloak and looked through the door.

"I brought you some victuals. Mair said I should be careful. I'd get whipped if I was caught."

"Cam, you're so kind. I was hungry. I fell asleep, you know." A bundle was passed through the door.

"The animals are all fine. Did you like Blaeno? I'd better go now."

Cam disappeared. This was an enormous boost to Cunval's spirits; with such friends in the community, he may be able to survive these fearful events. Singing while he ate, he examined his mud walls. Tomorrow, he would make some lime and give them a coat of lime-wash, just as he had seen at Tidiog's hut. What about the farm-work? Would he be expected to work as normal? He would have to walk on the moor, and give the matter some serious thought.

That night, the moon was full and the stars bright. Cunval walked and walked across the moor. He could see the outline of the hills to the west. Beyond them lay Caerleon, his spiritual home, the holy place where he had decided to devote himself to the good of mankind, where he had been baptised, and where he had found the meaning of true comradeship. The firm friendship of his fellow pupils seemed so distant now. They were all being prepared to go out into the country and spread the word of God, but the beliefs of the pagan world were so entrenched, and the power of frail young priests like him was so little.

This was a time for reflection. Cunval had hardly had time to think since his arrival. He was feeling sorry for himself, and that was very selfish. His bruises hurt, but his image of Jesus soothed the pain. His thoughts gradually turned to others, who had worse problems: his sister and her friend, who were captives; his brother, who had to face battle; the labourers, who were treated as slaves. His life was blessed compared with theirs. He had his own enclosure, food, friendship and the love of God. By first light, his heart was lifted; he strode across the moor, singing loudly. His path was quite clear. He would apologise to Brockvael and the clan, and ask for their forgiveness. If they beat him, so be it.

Mentally prepared, Cunval completed his morning chores and set off down the hillside. He could see that the settlement was stirring and, once on the bridge, he could see the warriors on horseback, preparing for a hunt. He could now either turn left for the hall, or walk onto the field to try to see Catvael.

He walked towards the warriors. A horse wheeled from the group and sped towards him. Should he shut his eyes and hope? Arteg harshly pulled up his horse to confront a nervous and apprehensive Cunval.

"There was a meeting last night, after Freid and Brockvael had a shouting match. The decision was that you are banned from the stockade. Brockvael does not want to see you there."

Obviously, Catvael had sent Arteg. Cunval could sense that he was a reasonable man; he had probably saved the priest's life when Catvael wanted to spear him.

"Thank you, Arteg. Bless you." Cunval looked intently into his eyes and then he was gone.

This was very embarrassing. Brockvael knew this would diminish Cunval's standing; effectively, he would be outside the community and shunned by the clan. Much more distressing was the thought of the children being turned against him. Would they be stopped from speaking to him? Cunval had decided to walk around the stockade to the fields, when a whooping gang of children came out of the gateway and ran up to him, laughing.

"Never mind, Cunval, we can help you." Olwen took his hand to comfort him. This was a blessed relief; the children had not been brought into the controversy. "Auntie Freid said to give you this pebble, and you would understand."

Cunval looked down at the bright, flat pebble. It was a

type of stone that he had not seen before. It was carefully inscribed with the Christian sign of the fish. Freid was saying sorry for having caused so much trouble for Cunval. He thanked Olwen.

"We'll come with you, Cunval," said Rees reassuringly. "Are you going to the fields to weed the corn?"

Thus, the scene was set for the next phase of Cunval's mission. He could carry on as before, but as an outcast of the settlement. Henbut and the labourers were still going to be his best friends, but they could not disobey the Yarl and make the young man welcome in their home.

June progressed and Rees grew closer to Cunval. They spent time together, enjoying their surroundings. Cunval showed Rees how to call foxes with the imitation of a wounded animal's cry, how to whistle to a song-thrush and get a reply, and how to make refreshing drinks from various plants. The countryside and the river were thronged with wildlife, and Rees came to love the animals rather than hunt them. Fishing, however, was an obsession with them both. Cunval had made his fish traps to be more and more elaborate, whilst Rees, with the regular training that he was receiving from Catvael, had become proficient with a bow and arrows. He was able to balance in a suitable tree and shoot trout in the river below. Cunval had to build his own smokehouse, and all types of fish were hard-smoked and ready for the cold winter months.

Rees had partly outgrown the younger children. With his teaching from Cunval and his evolving prowess with the warriors, he little realised that his destiny was one day to be warrior leader of the clan. Catvael, naturally, was uneasy about Rees' close friendship with Cunval, but he could see that Rees was learning many useful skills. Cunval felt, in some ways, that both he and Catvael had assumed the responsibility for Rees' upbringing. After all, Rees was of the clan bloodline, and, one day, he could be a tribal leader of great influence.

The summer was a time of enjoyment, but the calm was to be short-lived. A hue and cry went up one morning. A cow and calf had been stolen in the night. The warriors were furious. This was a personal insult to them, and no stone would be left unturned until the thief was caught. Some tracks led off into the king's woodland and the hills to the west, and if the thief got far enough away, then any pursuers would have to seek the king at Caerleon and obtain permission to follow in his tracks. By this time the thief could be hidden anywhere.

In the late afternoon there was a shout from across the fields. "They've got him. They're on the way back."

Cunval and the workers dashed to the track-way alongside their field. Catvael and some of the warriors rode past on their way to the hall, and following behind them was a hooded man, roped behind a horse. The cortege was closely followed by the cow and calf. The thief had obviously been badly beaten, and he staggered along in much pain. Cunval felt sorry for him, but could not understand how he could have been so stupid as to steal. Henbut thought he might be an outcast from another territory and, perhaps, lived in the hills alone.

"What will his punishment be, Henbut?" Cunval suspected the worst and it would be his duty to try and mediate.

Henbut looked at Cunval sternly. "Nothing can save

him. He will be tied to a stake overlooking the big pool and, tomorrow morning, he will be shot with arrows. His body will be weighted with large stones, and he will be thrown into the deep water, for the spirits of the ancestors to deal with him."

Cunval was horrified. "Thou shalt not kill," echoed through his mind. It was one thing to kill in battle, defending your family, but to kill a thief in cold blood was barbaric. Surely, he could be jailed at Abermenei and given the chance to repent.

After work, Cunval went to the big pool, where Durwit was chanting, whilst the warriors practised their archery. The miserable thief, tied to a stake, was terrified and sobbed uncontrollably. Cunval could see that his face and chest were badly bruised. As he got closer, Cunval froze; it was Mocan, the thief who had tried to rob him on the road from Caerleon. The warriors glared as Cunval approached them.

"Catvael, please spare this poor man. He made a terrible mistake."

Catvael was exasperated at this bold intrusion and ordered his men to throw Cunval into the river. There could be no further discussion. Once more, with wet clothes, Cunval climbed the pathway to his hut with a heavy heart.

Later, pacing the moor in the dusk, Cunval knew that there was only one course of action for him. He could not stand by and allow a fellow human to die. When the evening carousing had died down, Cunval crept to the river-bank, where he could just see Mocan in the gloom. He sat and listened. If Durwit was around, he would move at some point. Cunval waited for a long time before wading the river and crawling to the slumped figure at the stake.

"Don't make a noise. I'm a friend." The wretched thief tensed and grunted as Cunval took his arm. "I'm going to set you free, but you must promise me that you will never steal again. If you do, you will surely die next time."

"I promise. I promise." Cunval was in no doubt that Mocan had learnt his lesson. Unable to untie the tight bonds in the darkness, Cunval used a sharp flint knife that he had brought in anticipation.

"I've brought you some food. You must cross the river and run over the moor. When you come to a big river, cross it and keep going until you come to Caer Gloy. Ask to see the bishop there."

"Who are you? Why should you help me?"

"I am the priest of Penhal. I cannot stand by and watch you die. Go now, and God be with you."

Mocan slumped to his knees, his muscles cramped from his injuries and the tight bonds. Cunval helped him to the river, then he was gone.

chapter 14

It was dawn when the cry went up, "The prisoner has escaped!" As the furore died down, the workers were ordered to carry on in the fields, so Cunval waited for his colleagues at the south gate. He made a point of avoiding contact as they toiled through the day. The warriors had ridden off in all directions; some had gone to conduct a search of the moor.

On returning from the fields that evening, Arteg rode up to confront the workers. This was a surprise to the others, but Cunval had fully suspected to receive bad news.

"You are all summoned to the hall, you also, Cunval. Brockvael is waiting." Arteg looked into Cunval's eyes; his expression was not one that Cunval could recognise.

Henbut shook his head. This meant trouble, especially if Brockvael had been drinking. Cunval had not been allowed into the hall for some time, and he hoped Freid was still in good health. When they all walked through the main enclosure there was not a soul in sight. The reason was soon apparent: the whole community was squeezed into the hall. This was a meeting of great importance.

Cunval was pushed roughly to the front. Brockvael, who was unsteady on his feet, glared at him.

"Stand there and wait." He jabbed at Cunval with a trembling finger. Cunval felt someone squeeze his hand; he looked down hopefully, and Freid smiled up at him, but her expression was tense.

The crowd parted as Durwit entered, clad in his usual hideous attire. He stood by Brockvael, as his master spoke.

"The prisoner did not escape last night. He was set free. See, all of you, the ropes have been cut with a knife. You, priest, are you the guilty one?" Brockvael was almost shouting as all eyes turned to Cunval.

"Yes, sire. I cannot allow a man to be killed. It is against all the laws of my God. I would rather be killed myself than witness that poor man's death." Cunval's voice faltered with fear, and Freid squeezed his hand even harder.

Durwit was beside himself with anger. At last he would see the back of Cunval. "The priest must die. He must stand in place of the thief. It is the law!"

Cunval had been brooding all day. If this was to be his last day on earth, then he was justified in not owning up to the release of the prisoner that morning. However, as a man of the cloth, he could have done nothing else. His fate was now with his God.

One of the warriors offered his drunken advice.

"The priest should be flogged first. In the old days, he would be blinded and killed slowly."

Durwit shouted abuse in full support. The rest of the community looked shocked. They had not suspected that Cunval could have released a common thief. The children were crying and the younger women sobbed. They just could not comprehend that Cunval might die. They knew that if Brockvael shouted "death" nothing could save him.

All heads turned as Brockvael's older wife, Gwenhaen, rose slowly to her feet. Surely she would not dare speak. She had never raised her voice in front of them.

"I beg my husband not to be hasty." Brockvael looked uneasy as she turned to Catvael and his warriors. "I well remember your grandfather, the great Morval. He was a fine man and, near the end of his life, he became a good Christian, just like Cunval and Freid. Henbut and Mair knew him well; he was a fair man as well as a great warrior."

There was silence, apart from Durwit's heavy breathing and shifting feet. Gwenhaen continued. "He would not avenge an act of mercy with death. Brockvael, can I beg you, please, to spare Cunval? Banish him to the other side of the river. The king would approve, I'm sure of that!" Anhared helped her to sit down.

Was the surprise of Gwenhaen's speech and the persuasion of her argument to be the answer to Cunval's prayer? The older wife knew Brockvael better than anybody, and she had obviously touched a nerve as she had risen to this occasion. Brockvael certainly did not want Cunval's death on his conscience if it unfavourably altered the balance in the community. Rees might never forgive him as long as he lived. Worse still, his old friend, the king, was known to be a Christian supporter, and might strongly disapprove if Cunval were mistreated.

"You are banished. Go!"

Brockvael had barely spoken when Catvael lurched forward. Cunval gulped; his thoughts numbed.

"Let me speak. This priest must not be able to get away with this crime; he must be punished severely!" His men stood back. "He has tried to corrupt our children with his one God. Yet, we have been victorious in the past, with the help of our true gods. Mars is our god of war; Maponus has protected our beloved valley from the beginning of time;

even the Romans did not come to this place. Every wellspring that gushes into this valley is an embryo god, produced by the mother earth to be nourished by dear Lupicina, our own goddess of the Menei. She, in turn, flows to Diva, the goddess of the Gwei, and when the Gwei reaches the mighty Hafren, holy Sabrina herself rides on her waves to the feet of the great gods in the west."

Catvael's speech was emotional and full of pagan conviction. Cunval was once more shaking. In his rage, Catvael had pulled Cunval toward him and now, uncontrollably, he butted the young priest with his forehead. The stabbing pain and the agony in his head caused Cunval to lose consciousness. This was, no doubt, the best thing that could have happened. Cunval was now laid out on the floor, with blood spurting from his smashed nose. The fussing of the women and the shouts of the children ended the gathering of the clan.

A moaning Cunval was carried to Henbut's house, where he spent the night in great discomfort. He prayed and prayed to try and relieve the pain, and could only grunt and breathe through his mouth. Nevertheless, he knew that he had survived for the time being; surely they would not want to kill him now. Perhaps the recovery of the cow and calf would help his case. He was certainly indebted to brave Gwenhaen as well as his all-seeing God.

The next morning Cunval was helped to his hut. Brockvael had given orders that Cunval was to be banished to the other side of the river. He was to be responsible only for the cattle and sheep on the moor, and on no account was he to teach the children of the Christian religion.

For several days Cunval hardly left his hut. He felt very

ill and wondered if he would ever recover. Rees and Henbut visited and brought him broth and milk. He could not chew and he could hardly see; even breathing was so difficult. He hid his swollen face and wondered what shape his nose would be, if it healed at all.

Cunval's convalescence was a blur. He was able to send messages to Gwenhaen and Freid, and it appeared that the whole community thought him a complete fool to risk his life for a thief, but they were so glad the crisis was over.

After two weeks, the headaches had subsided and Cunval was able to walk the moor and the woods. He hoped the thief was safe and had reformed. It seemed that they had both been given a second chance.

As he could not now do farm-work with the labourers, Cunval busied himself with the construction of a new corral on the moor. He sited it out of the north wind, and it was so high and solid that even marauding wolves could not enter. Each night, the cattle came to the old corral and, with an armful of fresh grass to tempt them, they were easily persuaded to go on to the new enclosure. The cattle were small and black. A handsome bull was the leader, and nine of his ten cows now had well grown calves. They were quite separate from the mixed herd in the fields behind the settlement, which were kept for milk. Good bull calves were exchanged with the other farms, sometimes far afield. Cunval liked the notion of sharing.

Cunval's garden was immaculate once more and all of the new vegetables would soon make a welcome addition to his diet. The large garden behind the settlement was also well looked after, and Henbut kept Cunval informed of all the farming activities. Although he was sometimes very depressed with his circumstances, Cunval remained quite cheerful in company and could only hope that time would heal the rift between himself and the community across the river.

One glorious summer's evening, Rees and Hawk came running up the pathway. Rees had a grim face.

"Cunval, Freid is dying, her mind has gone and she will not eat. She keeps saying she wants to go home."

Cunval was in a panic. He had not considered that Freid would become ill so suddenly. On their trip down-river, Freid had been obsessed with having a fine Christian burial in Cunval's new cemetery. He wondered if he should go down to the bridge. Brockvael would have plenty to say about this.

"Grandma Gwenhaen sent me, Cunval. She said she will meet you presently, down by the river. I'll walk down with you."

Cunval put his arm around Rees' shoulder as they walked.

"Everybody has to die some time, Rees. I know you and Olwen have become very fond of Freid. She's a dear old lady."

Gwenhaen stepped gingerly across the bridge to meet them.

"Cunval, I do think the end is near. Brockvael has gone hunting for a few days and he expects Freid to be gone when he gets back. He had agreed when she first came here that she could be buried in your enclosure; even Durwit did not want her remains in the big pool."

"I'm so glad of that, but I'm not sure what to do. I dare not go to the hall but, instead, I'll say prayers for her here." Cunval knelt, facing the Penhal commune, and both

Gwenhaen and Rees lowered their heads as Cunval prayed in Latin.

"I'll get word to you, Cunval."

Gwenhaen climbed back onto the bridge. It was so good for Cunval to have contact again, and he and Rees retraced their steps up the pathway.

As dusk was approaching, Cunval and Rees strolled onto the moor, to check the returning animals. Rees now had his own staff, which he had fashioned from a stout branch of wych elm. Cunval had erected a brushwood and stake fence across the front part of the moor, to enclose the sheep and their lambs. This gave them plenty of summer grazing, and he had cut down some of the heather and gorse to encourage the growth of more new grass. However, when he tended the sheep, he would let them out further onto the moor, for a few hours of fresh grazing. The cattle were no trouble at all. No matter how far they roamed, they would always return in the early evening for Cunval's freshly-gathered grass and, of course, their water trough was filled from Cunval's spring.

The sheep had already entered their own section of the corral, and the cattle walked homewards as Cunval and Rees strolled across the moor to count them in. There was a distant howling that alerted Cunval to a possible danger; it sounded like wolves on a chase. Cunval started to run along the main pathway that led over the moor, followed by Rees and Hawk. Was one of the new calves being attacked? Cunval thought that he had counted them all. There had never been trouble with wolves before, they rarely ventured from the mountains in the north.

The noise came from a hollow where the cattle sometimes

sheltered from the sun and, as they approached, it was obvious that wolves had trapped an animal. Cunval with Hawk was well ahead of Rees and, as he charged through the bracken to some fallen trees within the hollow, he saw two young male wolves snapping at an old dog that was crouched under a thorn bush.

With loud shouts, that surprised Cunval himself, he ran into the fray and swiped at the surprised wolves with his staff. Hawk lunged at this hated enemy, lips curled and snarling, and then Rees appeared over the brow of the hill, shouting like a mad man. The wolves yelped and turned tail: a barking dog and two demented humans had unnerved them. They disappeared over the hillcrest.

"Phew! I've never seen wolves before." Rees was delighted at this triumph. "I've heard them sometimes. They're not so fierce, are they?"

Cunval realised that, without thinking, he had led Rees into what could have been a dangerous situation. Suppose there had been a whole pack of wolves. It did not bear thinking about. Cunval was surprised at his own aggressive behaviour. He had never acted like this before. His time at Penhal had changed him from a timid and nervous young man into an impetuous gladiator.

"This old dog's been bitten, Rees. We must get away from here. There may just be other wolves about."

The dog whimpered as Hawk sniffed at him. He struggled to his feet, but his rear legs were damaged and his ear and cheek had been bitten. Cunval managed to cradle him in his arms and they all set off for home. A log enabled Cunval to rest half way, and Rees and Hawk ran on to check the cattle and sheep. Eventually, Cunval entered his hut, exhausted from the effort, and proceeded to make the old dog as comfortable as possible on his bed.

"It will be dark soon, Rees. I'll walk down to the bridge with you, and you can tell Henbut all about the danger. He will probably want to send one of the labourers up here, to help stand guard tonight."

"Yes, and when our Catvael gets back, he'll soon hunt those wolves down!"

chapter 15

Just as Cunval had predicted, the children were early coming to his hut. They wanted to nurse the new dog and make him better. The injured dog had instinctively licked his wounds, eaten some bread and fish, and now lay stretched out in the sunshine at Cunval's doorway. It looked as if he would recover in a few days. Hawk ran up, whimpering and with tail wagging, and licked the wound to the dog's ear.

"Here, boy! I've got a bone for you."

The old dog gently took the bone from Olwen's outstretched hand. Olwen then gave a bone to Hawk, to avert any danger of jealousy. They all stood clear as the old dog managed to gnaw, despite his injuries.

Olwen turned to Cunval. "There, I knew you wouldn't have any meat or bones." Cunval shrugged; he knew that the girl considered him inadequate when it came to some of the practical things in life. As a man who ate no meat, how should he have bones? Olwen continued, "You were very brave, Cunval, seeing off those wolves."

"I wouldn't have dared it without Rees there," replied Cunval, "and Hawk tried to bite them, too."

"Well, anyway, I think you were very brave to canoe on the big pool and to let that thief go free. Nobody else would have dared do that."

Cunval fingered his misshapen nose. "I couldn't help it

really, Olwen. The circumstances were beyond my control. I can't control my own fate, if you can understand what I mean."

"Sort of. Did your God save you, Cunval?"

"Well, I suppose so, but you know that I'm not allowed to speak of my God at the moment. I'm sure all this trouble will be forgotten in time."

"Now," said Olwen, who seemed to have taken charge, "What are you going to call the dog, Cunval? I wonder where he came from. Do you think he was banished because he was old?"

"Possibly, Olwen. I think you children should give him a name, though."

"Durwit," offered one of the younger children, and raised a laugh. Cunval thought that, before his arrival at the settlement, they would not have dared to make such fun.

"I helped to save him!" Rees stroked the old dog and said, "I think we should call him Wolf."

This sounded sensible and they all agreed. The newly named dog, Wolf, rolled over as they made a fuss of him. He was obviously well acquainted with children.

Cam had been sent by Henbut to keep a fire going all night at the corral, and Cunval had relieved him before dawn. After some sleep and checking the moor for any sign of the wolves, Cam took the children with him when he was ready to return to the settlement. Cunval intended to release the animals for the day and stay with them on the moor.

Cunval could not bear to be idle for long. He already had a plan for doing something useful if he was going to be stuck on the moor just watching the animals. He took his tools and some straight pieces of elm and, once the cattle and sheep were grazing peacefully, he set to work splitting the timber and making up thin cleft slats, to make a coracle for the children. The shallow pool, where they played and learnt to swim, had a raft and other logs to serve their games. Cunval thought they would be proud of a proper boat, but there was another purpose for making the framework. He intended to build a pottery kiln, and the shape of the coracle framework would be ideal for his purposes. The jars, bowls and dishes of the settlement were worn and cracked, and although new crockery was sometimes obtained through trade with Abermenei, the warriors regularly broke anything that got in the way of their drunken brawls.

Seeking out a large, flat-topped boulder as a work-bench, Cunval first made up an oval hoop from a sturdy slat. His brace and a jagged spike of metal enabled him to drill holes in the appropriate places, and he then bound the overlapping joint with bark strip. Soon, he had bent over the other slats to form a complete shell, each joint and cross-over point bound tightly.

Satisfied that it was rigid, he hoisted it over his head and carried it to the corral. This had turned out better than he had expected. As a coracle, it was going to be large enough for four children, and, with paddles, they would have great fun.

Cunval placed the shell on top of the heather to dry in the sunshine. He would next plan out his kiln and form a flat stone base raised up from the ground. On this he would stand the beehive-shaped shell of the coracle, upside down, and build the kiln around this framework, all in stone, and with a doorway for access. After the stonework was completed and set in position, he would be able to cut the bark binding strips and remove all the slats from inside his new kiln. When it came to re-building the shell as a coracle, he would use thin leather thongs in place of the bark and, with a goat skin covering, it would be ready for launching.

During his time at Caerleon, Cunval had taken an intense interest in all the activities that went on in the town. He and his fellow pupils would visit the boat-builders' yard, the carpenters' workshops, the smithies, the markets and the grand river tournaments. Although he had never built a pottery kiln himself, he had watched the potters at work, and they had allowed the young students to make their own pots and figurines. He was sure he could make it work.

The sight of Rees running up the pathway interrupted Cunval's thoughts. He somehow sensed that there was news of Freid.

"It's all right, Rees. I know what you're going to say." The expression on Rees' face had already relayed the message to Cunval. He took the boy in his arms to comfort him. "It's all right to cry, Rees. She was a good person, but we only have a short time on this earth, and Freid will be going to heaven."

Cunval thought he should change the subject. "See this, Rees!" Cunval showed Rees the shell for the new coracle.

"Oh, yes! That's just what we wanted: a coracle."

"First, I have a much bigger job to do. I must make a coffin."

"What's that? What's a coffin? "

"It's a sort of wooden chest to put a mortal body into and give the dead person a dignified exit to this world. Then, the person is buried in the ground in a Christian cemetery. I'll show you tomorrow."

Cunval well remembered the burials he had attended, when he was the same age as Rees. A burial was not a pleasant occasion, but children should not be too sheltered from the inevitable process of death.

"Now, Rees, I would be most grateful if you could tell Gwenhaen that Henbut will know all the arrangements that have to be made. Then, when Henbut has finished his day's work, could you say that I would like to see him here this evening? He will understand."

Rees took off down the pathway and Cunval gathered up his tools. In anticipation of Fried's demise, Cunval had set aside some prepared wood for making a coffin. The cleft oak had been stacked behind his hut, with stones as weights. He now had a few hours of daylight in which to cut and plane off the wood, then bind it to squared-off corner pieces. A young priest's training encompassed many skills, and Cunval's movements were deft. As the coffin was taking shape, Henbut arrived with Cam.

"What can we do to help, Cunval? This is the first Christian burial at Penhal. It's a good job that Brockvael and the warriors are away. There's no sign of Durwit. I think he may have gone with them."

"Thank you for coming, Henbut, and you, Cam. I'm just making up this coffin top, then I'll show you the bindings for it." They both watched carefully as Cunval completed his task. This was the first time Cam had seen a coffin, or even heard of a Christian burial. Cunval had placed the coffin on two trestles, to facilitate the construction, and now he stood back.

"There, do you see how the top can be fastened down? Now, I'm going to carve Freid's name in the top, and a cross inside a circle."

While doing this, Cunval said that they could take the coffin down to the mortuary with them, so that the women could place Freid's body inside, then they could seal it and leave it in the mortuary until morning. If Henbut and the labourers were then available to bring the coffin up to the cemetery, Cunval would hold a service with the burial.

Henbut nodded. "I expect Gwenhaen will want to come here, Cunval. Will it be alright for the children to come too?"

"Of course, if Gwenhaen agrees. I would be most glad for any of the community to come. I will have the grave dug ready and it will be all over quickly. Oh, here, take the trestles with you."

Cam hoisted the coffin onto his shoulder and they set off downhill. Cunval's mind was buzzing with the details. This was his calling, and the procedures must be correct. However, he could not decide where in the cemetery to dig the grave. He grabbed his spade and went to the high cross for inspiration. The new dog, Wolf, had struggled from the hut, as they were talking, and laid himself down near the fencing at the lower west side of the enclosure.

"That's it, Wolf. That's the spot for the grave." The dog rose slowly to its feet and ambled a short distance away, then flopped to the ground again and eyed Cunval with curiosity.

Cunval removed the turf and checked the size by pacing the length and width of the patch, then stood back to be sure that the alignment was east to west. Soon, he was well down into the ground, and the excavated soil formed a huge mound to the one side.

Chapter 16

At first light and with the dawn chorus in full spate, Cunval sat up in bed. He was disturbed at having suffered his usual dreams. If ever there was something to worry about, Cunval's night-time dreaming accentuated his fears. In the night he had pictured the funeral with everything going wrong, with Durwit mocking him, and with the warriors on their horses smashing through his fences. He tried to shake off his feelings of doubt and get on with the preparations.

A slight drizzle was not going to help. The sky was now overcast and dull, and Cunval had to pick his way carefully down the pathway to avoid slipping. His cloak kept him dry while he waited at the foot of the bridge, where a large alder tree gave him some shelter.

Presently, voices at the settlement told him that he would not have to wait long. The women, including Helga, filed out through the east gate, and Cunval was surprised at the size of the congregation. The children and the old folk followed on with Henbut and Mair, and then came the coffin, borne on the shoulders of the labourers. The whole community had turned out to accompany Freid to her final resting-place. Cunval had no need to worry about the coffin coming safely over the narrow bridge. The labourers simply walked down the rough steps to the river's edge and waded across, to be greeted by Cunval.

"If you come to the bottom of the path, I'll ask the others to follow in procession."

Cunval now started to fuss and fret. He greeted the others off the bridge and lined them up in what he thought should be a correct order, with the old folk having the support of the younger women. He then scrambled past the labourers, to get to the head of the procession, ready to give the word to commence.

The procession up the now slippery pathway was a trial in itself; the coffin lurched once or twice, and Cunval slipped to the ground while trying to steady the labourers. On entering the cemetery, Rees stepped to the front and placed the trestles appropriately while Cunval ushered the labourers to set the coffin beside the grave.

A low whimpering caused Cunval to look around, wondering if Hawk had suddenly arrived on the scene. Rees was pointing into the newly dug grave. Cunval edged forward and looked down. A confused Wolf was looking up at him, and there was a hedgehog curled up in the corner. The labourers bent forward to peer into the grave and, without any prompting lifted Cunval by his arms and lowered him into the deep, damp pit. He struggled to hold up Wolf whilst trying not to hurt his wounds, and eased him out of the grave. Next, he lifted the hedgehog in both hands and scooped him up to the waiting helpers. Cunval was visibly flustered as he was then dragged out of the grave, wet soil spread down his tunic. He placed two stout poles across the grave.

"We will say prayers first."

Cunval conducted the Latin service and then turned to the congregation. "I'm afraid you won't understand the

Roman tongue; suffice it to say that the soul of our dear companion Freid is committed to God's care."

Cunval then gave a description of Freid's life and her contribution to the family. He motioned the labourers forward and helped them to fix two ropes to the coffin. As it was lowered into the grave, Cunval continued with his service and, at the conclusion, Cunval placed an inscribed wooden cross at the head of the grave, where he had prepared a small hole.

"Thank you all for coming. I know that Freid would have much appreciated your presence. If you want to come back and place flowers at any time, you will be most welcome." Cunval stepped back, to signify that the interment was now over, and the congregation slowly dispersed.

Cunval's first Christian burial was finished. He shut Wolf in the hut and encouraged the hedgehog out of the enclosure.

"We'll fill in the hole for you, Cunval. Have you got a hoe and a spade?" Cam's offer was most appreciated, for Cunval was now feeling tired after his night's toil.

"Thank you, Cam. Well, Henbut, do you think I'll make a priest? I was a bit nervous, you know."

"You've done exactly what Freid wanted, Cunval. Mind you, there's a few of us getting older around here, so you might be in for a busy time," Henbut said, smiling.

Cunval grimaced at Henbut's humour.

"I dare say I'll be next!" piped up Cam, causing the labourers to laugh. "Still, it's a nice spot up here!"

The grave was back-filled, and Cunval planned the array of wild flowers that he wanted to plant in the fresh earth.

He had marked the location of primroses and daffodils, in the late spring, before they faded, so that he could transplant some inside his enclosure.

That evening, Brockvael and the warriors returned from their hunting trip in the mountains. Cunval heard the hubbub across the river and hoped that the completed funeral had suited Brockvael's planned absence. The sound of wild, abandoned drinking and the smell of roasting wild pig wafting up from the hall meant that Cunval could have an early night.

Whilst tending the animals next morning, Cunval heard the sound of thundering hooves coming up to the moor. He was afraid that he might be in trouble again. Without stopping and hardly glancing at him, the warriors galloped past, followed by the pack of hunting dogs. They were, no doubt, going to hunt down the two wolves. He felt a surge of relief.

Rees followed on excitedly. "I think Arteg must like you, Cunval. He said you were brave to have a go at those wolves."

Cunval had already seen compassion in Arteg's eyes; not every warrior was a fierce pagan.

"Let me show you what I'm planning, Rees. I'm going to make a pottery kiln. I think you're going to enjoy this." They set off down the hillside below the crag and came to a level spot a little way up from the river.

"This is where we'll build up the kiln, but, first, we must look for some suitable clay. There should be some showing in the river-bank. You do enjoy squelchy mud, don't you?"

Cunval had thought to bring his spade with him and

tried several places in the search for a suitable hard clay seam.

"This could be the stuff, Rees. First, I'll dig a shallow pond through this pebble beach, and you can splash water from the river into it."

This done, Cunval then dug out lumps of clay, dropped it into the pond and cut it up with his spade. While Rees joyfully splashed water, Cunval tested some of the clay in his fingers and gradually worked it into a pliable ball.

"This will be fine. It needs to soak while we build up the kiln. I think it will take us quite a few days."

The children were playing up-stream, on the opposite bank, when they spotted Rees splashing in the river.

"Do you need some help, Rees?" The children ran excitedly down the bank, took off their boots and waded across in a shallow spot. Cunval took off his sandals and stepped into the muddy pond.

"How about a game, children? What we're trying to do is to squelch up all this clay in the pond, so that it turns into a smooth mud."

The children needed no encouragement; they all jumped into the pond and pounded away with their bare feet. This was so efficient that Cunval was able to add more clay.

Eventually, the job was done and everybody then washed in the river. It was time for Cunval to make some mint broth and share his honey cakes, so they all trooped up to the hut.

"Shall we pick some flowers for Freid's grave, Cunval?"

Olwen's suggestion was like music to Cunval's ears. He had been worried about the children's reaction to the grave in his enclosure. A cemetery was certainly not a normal part of their environment, but they had obviously accepted the situation. The children soon had armfuls of flowers and ferns, and by the time they had spread them over the exposed earth mound, the grave could not be seen. Wolf was now much better, and he loved the attentions of the children. After refreshment and an inspection of Cunval's neat garden, they all decided to walk on the moor. The animals needed to be checked, and they wondered if the warriors had found the wolves.

Of course, the children soon discovered the shell of the new coracle, and Cunval left it to Rees to explain the many intricacies of the kiln project.

"When can we start, Cunval. Can we do it today?" Olwen and the children were anxious to help with the collection of stones, and, so, throwing them down the hillside turned into a game. Cunval, meanwhile, was able to loosen more stones with the aid of his trusty spade.

"Careful, now. Don't rush, or someone may get hurt." Cunval had to restrain the children as the stones were hurled down the hillside into the wood.

"I haven't seen so many rocks since I was last at the seashore." As Cunval said this he realized that the children would now want to know all about the sea. He remembered the magic of his own family taking him to the beaches and the coves.

"What's it like at the seashore, Cunval? Can you take us there? How big are the fish?" The questions rained down on Cunval, who held out his hands and laughed. He motioned the children to sit down on the grass.

"When you're older, I would love to take you to the coast. The sand stretches for miles and miles, and the sea itself goes out with the tide and then comes back in with huge waves, and you have to run fast if you don't want to get swallowed up."

Cunval continued with his description of the cliffs, the rock pools, the crabs, the fish and the seabirds; all with enough exaggeration to keep the children spellbound. He knew that he was forbidden to talk of religious matters; that was his firm promise to Brockvael. However, he felt that he was now very close to the children, and it was his duty to lead by example.

They went home for supper, dancing wild pirouettes and chattering all the way down to the bridge.

Later in the evening, Wolf walked with Cunval onto the moor. The farm animals would now almost put themselves away, and the goat would follow Cunval around until he was ready to close up the corral. All was peaceful.

For the second time that day, Cunval heard horses in the distance, and he crossed to the track-way where they would have to pass. Catvael came into sight first, leading his men as usual, and Cunval lowered his eyes. He had, of course, forgiven Catvael for his enraged attack and, apart from his misshapen nose, he had put the incident out of his mind. Wolf started to growl as Catvael reined back on his horse and stopped.

"I'm sorry, sire. I don't know why he should growl."

Catvael laughed loudly and turned his mount for Cunval to see a dead wolf strung across the back of the horse. The wolf looked so beautiful. It was a magnificent animal. Its fur was sleek, and only a little blood around its mouth suggested that it had breathed its last. Cunval stepped back and shuddered as the warriors laughed at his weakness.

"We caught up with them at a farm near the Gwei. They had killed and eaten a calf." This was the first time Catvael had really acknowledged Cunval, and he was flattered.

"The big one got across the river and we lost him," offered Arteg. "He won't come around here again!"

"Oh!" Cunval could only nod. "Well, all of our animals here will be safe now. Thank you." He motioned towards his corral.

"Hmm." Catvael nodded approval of the sturdy enclosure and rode on.

It was time for some serious singing. The warriors seemed to have forgiven Cunval; his banishment from the settlement, and then his acceptance as part of the community, had come about as the result of a clash between paganism and Christianity. At this stage, it was as much as he could hope for, and time was on his side. He wondered whether the warriors would notice the flowers and the grave as they rode past his enclosure. He knew for sure that they would laugh at the newly made scarecrow in his garden.

Chapter 17

High summer was a time of plenty; there was an abundance of fish and vegetables, and harvesting of the field beans had begun. The wheat was starting to ripen and the orchard was going to produce much fruit. The women had started to collect cherries, plums and currents to make preserves, and it was now up to Cunval to produce more pottery jars. Butter and cheese-making had also diminished the supply of pots.

Rees and the children were keen to help Cunval with his kiln, and when it was finished, he could then make them the promised coracle. Cunval had cleared a flat area for the base of his kiln and the coracle shell was placed ready for him to build up a base of large stones in an oval around it. Much more clay was now needed. Once again, the children were able to play with sticky mud, and, after Cunval had cleaned off an area of smooth bedrock by the side of the river, the children scooped up the clay from the pond and spread it onto the cleared rock surface. It would dry off and produce the potters' clay that Cunval would require.

"Let me do the digging," said Rees, marching to the bank. Cunval transferred the spadefuls of clay to the now empty clay pit, and the children scooped water from the river into it. The whooping and screaming brought the women from the settlement to see what game was causing so much noise. Gwenhaen stood well clear of the splashing water, and Cunval was surprised to see Helga as part of the family group. She had been harvesting with the women, Cunval knew, and this was a good sign that she had now been accepted, even though Catvael was still very protective and jealous. Helga took a great interest in the proceedings and spoke to Cunval in her own language.

"For pots?" she asked, looking at the spread of clay.

"My kiln is up there," Cunval pointed. "Do you know how to make pottery?"

"Yes, of course. Are you going to make pretty jugs with patterns?"

"No. It would require too much heat. I can only make simple pots and things. I'm not an expert at all, you know."

Cunval motioned for the women to follow him to the base of the kiln and explained how he was going to build it up and make whatever size pots and bowls they wanted.

"We want to see how the animals are doing on the moor, and we want to see your corral." This was, indeed, pleasing to Cunval. The women had been forbidden to visit his enclosure until now, and it looked as if Gwenhaen had gained some influence on events. Perhaps Brockvael was slowly mellowing.

Cunval, as usual, ran rather than walked and he proudly skipped around the corral, showing the women how sturdy it was.

"If any more wolves come here in the night, they would never get at the animals, you know. I'm going to make a big shelter for the cattle before the winter. All the beehives are doing well. Will you be able to manage all the honey, when it's time to take it? We'll need lots of pails to carry it all down the hill."

"Now, don't worry, Cunval. Everything will be all right. You're such a fuss!" Gwenhaen gently shook Cunval's shoulder.

Brockvael's younger wife was laughing at Cunval. "Isn't he a chatterbox? Are all young priests like this?" The others chuckled and Cunval laughed readily with them.

Wolf had stayed at the enclosure, but, on hearing voices on the moor, he strolled over to meet everybody.

Anhared looked across the moor. "Whilst we're here let's go for a walk, shall we? It's such a lovely day."

The other women thought that was a good idea; they did not get much time for leisure.

"Cunval, show us where you and Rees rescued the old dog. Rees is quite a hero with the younger children," Anhared begged.

"And Brockvael says he's a chip off the old block," added Gwenhaen.

Wolf growled when they reached the hollow, so Cunval sat with him while he related the story, waving his arms about to add drama. Cunval spent a pleasant hour with the women. They planned the harvesting and storage, and, seeing the state of Cunval's tattered tunic, they decided to make him a new one before the winter. He would also require some more animal skins for his bed. He had spent little time in his life in the company of women, and their attention gave him a strange glow. This was somewhat disturbing, for he found their smiling eyes quite attractive.

There was a good harmony amongst the women, and Cunval was glad to see them all working together. He could see that there was a strange mixture: the older wife, the younger wife, the daughter-in-law, the Saxon woman from an enemy clan, and two lively younger women, wives of the warriors.

"Let me make you all some broth. I'll run on and get the fire going. I've made up a lovely mixture." Cunval ran towards his hut, glad of this chance to fraternise with the women. He had previously dried some pine twig tips, cherry flowers, herbs and lime seeds, and some of this mixture he always left soaking, ready for daily use. When the women arrived, they had already picked flowers for Freid's grave. Cunval set up his seating benches for them to rest, and this they were glad of after their long walk. Cunval always had a constant supply of honey cakes; the women were impressed with these, as Cunval had added a pinch of powdered honeysuckle.

Cunval gave the women a tour of his garden, and they promised to call again, to ensure that Cunval had enough butter and cheese.

When they walked on down the hill, chattering, and obviously happy with their sojourn, Cunval beamed with pride. His mission to the valley and his place in the community were now assured. He spent the rest of the day at work on the kiln, and, by the evening, he was weary but happy. He sang with gay abandon as he knelt in the vegetable rows, weeding. Then, without any warning, he sensed a presence and jumped up to go to the gateway. The last person he expected to see was Catvael, and with him was Helga. This did not mean trouble.

Catvael looked embarrassed.

"This woman is playing games with me. Ask her, yes, ask her in her own tongue, priest," Catvael coughed. "Ask her if she's expecting a baby."

As Catvael blurted out his request, Helga glared defiantly at Cunval. Although there was no discernible expression on her face, Cunval knew she was totally in charge of the situation. She well knew what Catvael was saying to him, and she was going to take full advantage of the situation.

"Yes, sire, I'll ask her." Cunval was overwhelmed. Here was Catvael openly asking for his advice. He was obviously obsessed with the notion of becoming a father, and unable to speak with Helga, other than by sign language, he had been driven to desperation.

"My lady, Catvael is anxious to know if you are going to have a baby." Cunval looked into Helga's eyes, but she turned away, tossing her hair. "Helga, I think Catvael likes you very much, and I think he wants to be a father."

Helga glided proudly into the garden and examined the neat rows. She picked some young field beans and fiddled with the pods. Catvael gave a sort of low roar. Cunval hoped he would not get into a rage and lash out. He tried to stand between Helga and Catvael.

"Talk, woman," shouted Catvael. "I must know."

Helga turned to Cunval, her eyes flashing.

"Tell him that I am a princess in my own tribe. I will not be treated like a slave. Ask him if he loves me and wants me to be his wife."

Cunval had difficulty in translating this to Catvael. He did not want to offend him but he knew that he must respect Helga's wording. He stumbled a little over the words but gave the message.

Catvael became exasperated. He could not back down, but neither could he run away from the situation. He turned to the gateway, muttering, and Helga berated him in the Saxon language. As they argued, Cunval stepped between them.

"I can marry people, you know!"

He realised this was the last thing he should blurt out, but it just happened. Catvael glared at him and turned on his heels.

"Ask him if he wants a boy, or a girl!" Helga shouted after him.

Cunval ran after Catvael. "Sire, sire, she asks do you want a boy or a girl?"

Catvael turned on his heels and stormed back up the pathway, nearly knocking Cunval over. He looked into Helga's eyes, which were still blazing. In a moment their arms were around each other and soon they were both sobbing. The tensions in Catvael had burst forth, and Cunval scuttled into his garden and shut the gate. He made a point of singing loudly, and waited until it was all quiet before peeping over the fence. They were gone, so it was time for supper. As he fastened his garden gate, he could just see the newly enlightened couple disappearing onto the moor. This was, indeed, a very satisfactory occasion, and to think that Cunval had been the catalyst for it!

The next two weeks were busy, but very happy. The betrothal of Catvael and Helga was anathema to Durwit, and Brockvael took a while to come round to the idea. Gwenhaen's new-found authority had mellowed Brockvael, who now spent more time away, hunting and visiting his outlying farms. Cunval was once more allowed to cross the river, but only to help with the harvesting and hay-making. In many ways, this suited Cunval; at least he was not in a position to upset anybody.

The main job for Cunval and Rees, when time allowed, was building up the top part of the kiln with the hard stones from the crag and clay from the pond. The original clay had been worked into a pliable mass, with coarse washed sand from the river mixed in. This would be for the pot-making. Henbut and the labourers gave a hand in the evenings, as the anticipation built up.

"This is fantastic," said Rees, as the kiln took shape. "I'll be able to make all sorts of pots and things."

Cunval had built up an extra ledge around the kiln, to enable him to stand up and reach the top of the dome. He then built in some suitable wedge-shaped stones, in order to leave an opening as a flue, and placed a thick flat stone on top as a smoke-vent.

"There you are, Rees. We can now take out the shell from inside. We just need to cut the bindings."

"Are you sure, Cunval, that it won't collapse?"

The children had gathered to watch this final phase. Cunval reached inside the doorway and, with Rees' knife, extracted the cleft slats of the coracle, one by one.

"Oh, no. It's all in pieces. It will never go together again."

Olwen was quite upset, but Rees knew better. They took the bundled slats and their tools down to the pebble beach and began re-assembling the coracle, this time with permanent strips of hide. Rees helped spread the three goats' hides that were to make up the skin of the craft, and Cunval, with much effort, started to stretch and sew the hides onto the frame. The jointing was waterproofed with animal fat mixed with dry moss.

It was quite some time before they were ready to start

the final phase: the fitting of a broad, wooden floor and two seats. The paddles had long been prepared.

Cunval was nervous when the time arrived for launching. They all proceeded to the head of the shallow pool, with Rees proudly carrying the new coracle over his head. He dropped it onto the water, where it rocked lightly, and the children waded in together, scrambling to get into the new boat.

"Wait, wait." Rees took charge. "Olwen, you and I can have a go next time, as we're bigger. You four get in first, carefully now, while I hold it."

The four smaller children gingerly climbed in, each pair face to face, while Rees held the coracle steady. Olwen passed the paddles to the awe-struck youngsters, who were now in charge of their destiny. They had all been taken for rides in the settlement canoes, but their very own boat was different. After turning in circles for a while, and rocking from side to side, Rees, who was firmly holding the coracle steady, pushed them out towards the start of the rapids. The water in the pool was no deeper than their waists, but Cunval stood in the shallows at the bottom of the pool, to be sure they made a safe passage.

"You're on your own now," shouted Rees, as the coracle picked up speed and with the four children wide-eyed and open-mouthed. They were soon shrieking with delight as their craft sped swiftly through the rougher water. All notions of paddling were forgotten and the coracle spun around out of control. They were still laughing when Cunval caught them and pulled them gently to the side of the pool. The children played for almost an hour in their new boat, until Cunval was exhausted.

"Look, Cunval," Rees was pointing upstream. "Here come Brockvael and Henbut. They're coming down to watch."

This was, indeed, a great honour; the children had started to get the hang of paddling, and Cunval thought to himself that Brockvael would surely approve. This exercise could well be construed as an early part of their military training, with a building-up of their confidence and character.

Sure enough, Brockvael smiled approvingly from the far bank and waved to the children.

"Would you like to try, sire?" Cunval thought a little humour might not go amiss, but Brockvael glared at him, stony-faced, and pursed his lips threateningly.

"He's thinking of drowning you!" laughed Rees.

Chapter 18

The most important time of the year had arrived and harvesting of the cereals consumed all thoughts. Even the warriors helped to bring the harvest into the settlement. They trailed the wheat sheaves from the fields on sledges behind their horses.

The storage barn for the grain had a raised wooden floor, which needed extensive repairs, and also the threshing floor was slowly collapsing. This was a chance for Cunval to ingratiate himself further with the clan. As a carpenter and with tools, it was conceded that he should carry out these repairs. Of course, he was to keep away from the hall.

The completed pottery kiln was now drying nicely in the hot sun and, after lighting a small fire, Cunval dried out the structure evenly, ready for the time when intense heat would be required.

Soon the harvest was done and the animals could be turned out onto the stubble of the wheat fields. Pottery was the next priority, and Cunval now felt himself indispensable to the community. While the threshing was going on, he and Rees constructed a small table on which to turn the clay.

With a low fire now burning constantly in the fire-box under the kiln, the time had arrived for making the pottery. The table was set up on the river-bank, and the children, seated on a bench, each had a lump of clay to knead. The moment of truth had arrived. The first item to take shape was a plain jar. A delighted Cunval worked feverishly, and, with Rees' help, soon got the hang of making pots and jars.

"Can I have a go?" asked Olwen. "And me?" echoed the other voices. Cunval was now faced with having to provide each child with some clay and instruction. Still, he was able to finish off each item with the aid of Rees, and soon there was a pottery collection of all sizes and shapes.

Cunval suddenly had an idea: the children could not read or write, and this was a subject that he hoped to address later. "I've got an idea," he said. You can each write your names on the mugs you have made, and it will stay there for ever."

The children looked glum. How could they write?

"Here, I'll show you how to do it." Cunval took a sharp stick and carefully wrote his name on one of the pots. "There, do you see? That's my name. Now, you next, Rees. I'll write your name on this flat piece of clay and then you can copy it onto your mug."

Rees concentrated hard and, with Cunval's help, his name took shape on the soft mug. Rees had developed a characteristic low whistle when he was learning from Cunval.

Each child, with Cunval's help, then inscribed their name on the mug they had made, and the rest of the clay was gathered up. A game then developed, to see who could make the best looking clay animal or bird. After several attempts, they each had a cherished object, and Cunval led them up to the kiln.

"Now, if we place this lot inside, on the floor of the kiln, the heat will dry them, ready for tomorrow, when we make up the fire again."

There was one more job to do back at the river. As the pots dried in the sun, more clay was dug and the game of splashing water into the pond got under way.

The women had walked down the river-bank, to watch the noisy proceedings, and were pleased to see the children having such fun. They were very impressed at the array of pots and mugs, and the writing caused much amusement. Cunval promised them that they could all have their names on pots, if the first firing was successful.

It was time for supper but, first, the children, who were already wet through, wanted to show their mothers how they could paddle their very own coracle. Once again, the air was filled with shrieking as the children paddled and swam.

"We've brought you some cheese, butter, bread and honey, Cunval." Anhared handed Cunval a basket; this was a welcome boost to Cunval's larder. He was never short of fish, and the summer's vegetables had given him much nourishment. Strings of onions had been dried and plaited, and the garden at the settlement that he had earlier planned and planted had given much food for winter storage.

Soon it would be time for the gathering of hazel nuts and chestnuts. Importantly, Cunval and Henbut were well versed in the art of making cider. Cunval knew that if he could make some large storage jars in his kiln, he could keep the cider fresher and longer than in the settlement's wooden barrels. There was so much to plan for.

Later, back in his hut, Cunval felt lonely. He had never lived on his own before; there had always been company. Ever since his banishment from the settlement, he had experienced nagging doubts about his inner strength. He knew that everything that had happened was a test put before him by God and, to some extent, he gained solace from his prayers and his constant memories of life at Caerleon. He knew that Wolf had been sent to him by some divine providence and, of course, a dog was a constant source of joy, but a sense of loneliness lingered at night-time. However, there were always means of staving off depression: singing and the preparation of food.

"It's time for supper, Wolf. Now, this evening, I think we might have some vegetable broth."

Cunval set a pot of water over his fire and went to the spring, followed by Wolf. He had constructed a recess at the back of the spring and built up a stonework chamber with a removable slab in the front. This acted as a cool store for his butter, milk and cheese. He took out a dish with the leftovers of fish from the day before.

"Here we are, Wolf, here's your supper. I think I'll have some cheese followed by honey. But first a bowl of broth."

Later, on the moor, the cattle and sheep had started to drift home and Cunval sat high on his fence and coaxed them in.

Strangely, his thoughts turned to Durwit. He had not seen the shaman for some time; he knew he had accompanied Brockvael on his occasional travels, but he had never shown up at the fields or gone onto the moor. Perhaps Durwit had the same feelings of loneliness as Cunval, he lived almost a mile upstream and was invariably on his own. Could Cunval allow himself any feelings of pity for Durwit? After all, underneath his evil exterior he was still a human being.

The next morning, after his usual duties, Cunval was off to the riverbank. He stopped at the kiln, to relight the fire, and checked that the clay animals inside the kiln were hardened off and ready for firing. As he walked on down the hillside and on to the pebble beach, his singing stopped abruptly. A branch had fallen down onto the collection of pottery and broken most of it. How could he have been so stupid? He should have made a cover of sorts, rather than leave the whole collection exposed overnight. Wolf, who had followed him, gave a strange low growl; he was saying something to Cunval. As he carefully peered around him, it dawned on Cunval that someone else had been there. He examined the footprints that he could now see were superimposed on his own small prints and those of the children. It could only be Durwit, who must have toppled a branch onto the collection of pots, to make it look like an accident, and it must have happened early that morning.

This was most frustrating and just when he thought Durwit would not strike at him again. There was no room for dejection; he would have to start again.

"Morning, Cunval. I see you couldn't wait to get into the pond!" Rees shouted from across the river, and, luckily, the children were not with him. Wolf barked a greeting and waded into the shallow water.

"There's been an accident, Rees. A branch fell onto the new pottery. We need to make some more, and I'd rather the children didn't know."

"Oh, no! Never mind, I'll set up the table. Are you making up some more clay?"

With the practice from the previous day, a new batch of mugs took shape. Cunval explained that they should make some spares and also get started on the bigger jars. After a hard day's work, they were both glad of some cool milk and cakes.

That night, Cunval slept near the kiln, under a calm, starry sky. He would be able to fuel the fire and stay alert for any intrusion. Wolf, knowingly, lay facing the pathway.

chapter 19

After a restless night spent stoking the fire and snatching some sleep, all wrapped up in his hide, Cunval dozed in the early morning sunlight. The dawn chorus was louder than he had ever remembered and he put his hands over his ears. However, there emerged another sound: men shouting down at the settlement. He stood upright and listened. He could hear the warriors shouting at their horses. What on earth could be the bother? Cunval felt a little frightened when Wolf started to bark.

Racing up through the wood to his hut, he intended to run down the pathway towards the bridge. From the pathway he would be able to see across to the settlement. As he strode up through the undergrowth to his enclosure, a horseman galloped up the pathway towards him. It was Cynvarch, the king's envoy.

"Sire, sire, what is the matter?"

"Pray for your warriors, priest. Pray hard and long."

The envoy, astride a magnificent white horse, wheeled and looked at Cunval's cross.

"I am Cunval, sire, a pupil of Bishop Dyfrig."

"Ah, yes, I recognise you. Well, Cunval, the Saxons are massing near Corinium and the king is collecting an army. Every good man is wanted." Cynvarch had obviously ridden hard from Caerleon.

Cunval was crestfallen at this news; people were going

to die. "Sire, is there news of my brother Cynan?"

"Yes, Cynan and his men will be gathering at Black Rock; the main army will cross the Hafren there and then march east. Everybody in the north will go to Caer Gloy for provisions and join the Cornovi cavalry." With that Cynvarch spurred his horse and made for the moor and the next settlement to the east.

"God be with you, sire," Cunval shouted after him, then, turning on his heels, he ran down the pathway, his thoughts in turmoil.

The tournament field was littered with weapons, packs and equipment of war. Cunval raced across the bridge and joined the children.

"Now, don't worry, I'm sure they will all come back safely." He could see that the younger children had tears in their eyes; they knew Rees and Olwen had lost their father in a battle with the Saxons, and now their own fathers were off to war.

Cunval ran over to Catvael. "Sire," he asked, "is there anything I can do to help? I know that I'm not much use but can I carry something for you?"

"Don't worry, priest. Your place is here. Look after the children. We'll be back within the week." Catvael was busy barking out orders. He was a born leader and tried to instil confidence in his band of men. Their constant training was soon going to be put to the test.

It was then that Cunval noticed Durwit, decked out with his wolf's head, smaller animal heads hung from his belt. He rode a horse and carried a spear and a sword decorated with feathers. If nothing else, he looked fearsome. His main job was to watch over Catvael, his leader. Brockvael firmly believed that his gods would keep his son safe in battle and, in some ways, Cunval felt that any faith was permissible in these circumstances.

"Are you going to pray for them, Cunval?" asked Olwen. "Will it help them to win?"

"I will certainly be praying for them. They're very brave and they'll watch out for each other."

Cunval would also pray for his brother, Cynan. He could remember Cynan, some years earlier, when he went off to war, full of bravado, but there were had been other warriors, many of them who did not come back at all. War was a terrible waste of life.

A fire had been started out in the open field and a feast was in preparation. The warriors would eat their fill and take with them, on a packhorse, as much as they needed. Large numbers of arrows were bundled together for the coming combat, and the clan well remembered how frightening it had been to watch the warriors shooting their arrows at the practice targets. The whole community helped and, by noon, it was time for the band to take their last wine and depart. Brockvael unashamedly hugged his son and then stood by with his arm around Gwenhaen. He could barely hold back his emotions.

Cunval scuttled up the pathway to his cross. The war band would be riding past his enclosure onto the moor and off to the east. As he knelt at his cross and prayed, the sound of horses drifted up the pathway. He stood at his gate and waited. The dogs appeared first, followed by the warriors, who sat proudly on their horses, their faces grim as they avoided looking down at him.

"God be with you," whispered Cunval, as each horse

passed by. The young man, Maervun, from Blaeno, now looking very pale and vulnerable, was particularly in his thoughts. Although he felt quite useless in such circumstances, Cunval decided to follow on behind the group, in a gesture of support. Wolf seemed to understand that this was not just a hunting party, and he followed his master, instead of trotting on in his usual manner.

With a little running, Cunval was able to traverse the moor and watch the group descend into the next valley before making for the Gwei. They would be at Caer Gloy on the River Hafren by nightfall. As they disappeared into the distance, Cunval once more sank to his knees.

It was now the duty of a priest to comfort the community. He would attend on the women, enquire if he could help with the chores, and would occupy the children with many games. In Cunval's experience, it could be weeks before the warriors returned; it would all depend on how well organised the Saxons were. If they had assembled a large army, it could be a serious matter. First, he needed to attend to his flock.

Gwenhaen and the women were still in the field when he approached.

"Can I help? Can I carry anything?"

"No, Cunval. We need something to occupy us for a while. It was a terrible shock to be woken early this morning by the king's envoy, and now all the men are gone."

"What if I take the children down river? That will interest them. They enjoyed the long walk up to the old settlement, and we can bring back some firewood."

"Yes, Cunval, I think that's a good idea, and if you take the labourers with you, I'm sure they would enjoy a long walk for a change."

"I'll go and see Henbut. It will probably suit everybody."

Soon, the walk down river was turning into a big adventure; the children responded to the idea of an outing with enthusiasm, and the labourers were glad of anything different from their normal hard toil. Some food was packed, and they all made for the bridge. Hawk joined in with old Wolf to form a hunting pack.

"There's something I want to show you lot," said Cunval softly. "If we walk along the hillside first, then we can drop back down to the river afterwards." He led the way for a short distance, then stopped and knelt on some fresh earth. "You see, a badger's set!" The children recoiled in fear and even the labourers stepped back warily.

"There are spirits down there, Cunval. You're not to touch it." Olwen scolded Cunval for such a dangerous game. The pagan beliefs were of earth spirits that came out at night and stalked the woods. Large poisonous snakes also lived in the deep burrows and, of course, only the shaman could protect the community from all of these underground devils.

"Nonsense," said Cunval lightly. "The only evil spirits are all in the mind." Cunval had promised not to teach the children of his Christian religion, but that had not excluded debunking pagan myths. "Here, I'll show you." To everyone's horror, Cunval lay down on the earthen mound, reached down into the largest hole, and started singing. He then poked his staff down as far as it would go and shouted at the top of his voice, "I curse you all, you loathsome impostors, and you odious snakes. You don't scare me. Oh, yes, you can frighten children. Come out tonight and see me at my hut. I dare you!"

What with Wolf and Hawk barking down the other badger holes, the children held their hands over their mouths in horror; they knew that Cunval could be quite mad sometimes, but this was playing with fire. The labourers looked quite stricken.

"I dare say you'll be a goner by the morning, Cunval." Cam, at least, rose to the humour of the occasion, and Cunval laughed loudly while the others shook their heads in disbelief.

"I think Cunval is right," stated Rees, sticking his chest out bravely. "Mind you, I would never do that myself!"

With the spirits suitably ridiculed, Cunval led the party on. Normally, he would not have been a confident leader, but in these circumstances he had an important job to do and felt quite proud that everyone looked up to him.

A scream from the girls gave Cunval quite a start. He dashed back to see a grass snake vanishing into a bush and, without hesitation, he grabbed the harmless creature by the tail and held it up. The whole company recoiled. Durwit had put them in fear of all snakes. Once more, Cunval gloated over Durwit.

"My brother cooks them on the fire and eats them," stated Cunval, trying to keep a straight face. He set the snake down and it vanished into the undergrowth.

When they returned to the riverbank, there was much for the children to examine. They lifted stones to look at the eels, crayfish and loach, and avoided weeds where leeches may by lurking. Trout and dace gobbled flies from the surface of the water, and ducks and moorhens broke cover noisily.

The labourers decided to untangle the larger lengths of firewood strewn on the bank and caught up in the alder trees. All was now ready for collection in the autumn.

After a while, Cunval judged that they had gone far enough for one day. They had finished up half-way to Abermenei and it was time for some refreshment. Rees took charge of making up a table with some driftwood, and the labourers eagerly helped. They knew that Rees was of the ruling family and were cheerfully respectful of him. Their life was simple; they had food and shelter and had no wish to take any responsibility. They would never want to be warriors; that was too much like hard work.

"I'll share the food out." Olwen, as usual, did not trust anybody else to undertake fairly such a delicate task.

Rees had chosen a sandy beach in the shade and the labourers stretched out. This was luxury compared to the heavy work they could normally expect during the day.

"Is Catvael fighting the Saxons yet, Cunval?" One of the younger children was bound to bring up the subject.

"No, not yet. They're all joining up to form a huge army. That way, everything should be all right. They'll probably be back in a few days."

Cunval thought that he would make light of the position to avoid worrying the children. He knew the situation was desperate; the Saxons usually raided in war bands and could normally be beaten off, but if they had amassed an army there would be a big battle and that would mean horrific bloodshed. The Saxons had few horses but were dangerous with their spears and long swords. A large Saxon army would be able to withstand the Celtic cavalry attacks, especially if they were on a hill. Cunval's brother, Cynan, had told him that if the Saxons took prisoners they would sacrifice them. He would pray hard every night until the warriors returned.

Rees pointed as he saw a heron land further up-river. "Let's see if we can creep up and watch him catch a fish."

This was a new game. Cunval had encouraged the children to watch the animals and birds secretly, hoping this would encourage them to respect nature and refrain from hunting just for sport.

Rees led the way and they all crawled along the sand and through the bank-side vegetation. The labourers and Cunval were obliged to follow on and the children gave them signals. Soon, with Rees' expertise, they were all lined up in the long grass, watching the heron wading in the shallows. The tall, grey bird took up a motionless stance and waited. Then, with a quick dart, it speared a minnow and raised its head to swallow it. Several more fish followed as the whole gang looked on enthralled, but, eventually, one of the younger children spoke too loudly and the heron took off in alarm.

"Never mind," said Cunval. "I think we'd better finish off the food, or throw it to the fishes. It's time to start upstream. I must see to the kiln soon."

With the camp-site tidied up, it was time to cross the river. The labourers became horses and the children were ferried across the river in a race.

"I'm the winner," shouted Cam. With Olwen, he had crossed in the shallower part and out-witted his colleagues. The dogs took off after a hare and, by the time the group caught up, Hawk had run it down. Cunval did not want to see Rees paunch it.

When they got to a marshy field, a large flock of lapwings

soared from the rushes into the sky.

"My favourite birds!" shouted Cunval with unashamed excitement. "Look, everybody, see how they twist and tumble in the air. They're the best flyers of all."

The children spread out their arms in imitation of the birds, and zoomed about the field, mimicking their twists and turns. Even the labourers, now tired, joined in, until the lapwings decided to fly away from these silly antics.

The trek up-river ensured that the children would sleep soundly that night, and the labourers, who were not used to so much walking, started to flag by the time the settlement came into view.

When they got to the shallow pool, the children were too tired to think of playing with the coracle, and this suited Cunval. "I'll cross the river here, everybody. Tomorrow, we can fire up the kiln and see what happens. What do you say?"

"See you tomorrow," shouted the children wearily as Cunval waded across the shallows with Wolf.

Chapter 20

After stoking up the fire under the kiln and arranging the pottery ready for firing, Cunval had several chores. The cattle and sheep, as usual, came to his calls, politely ignoring his constant chatter, and a quick walk over the moor ensured that they were all in. Next, he went to his garden and collected a snack of fresh carrots, onions and small turnips. The plants that he had allowed to go to seed, he lovingly caressed and told them of their important destiny. Wolf, now used to these strange rituals, lowered his head to the ground and sighed.

As the sun started to go down in the west, Cunval prayed at his cross. His thoughts were with the warriors, pagan or not, and he prayed for their souls and sang for their deliverance. Singing always helped to give him strength. Even so, as he rose to his feet an hour later, tears were streaming down his cheeks. He felt emotional and drained and helpless. Wolf seemed to understand and Cunval was so glad of the old dog's company.

He then thought it better if he spent the night at the kiln. He could keep the fire going gently all night and it would help to counter his thoughts of the war to the east. He took a large mug of broth, which he could re-heat over the kiln fire, together with some bread and cheese, and a hide to cover himself whilst he slept.

After a fitful night, Cunval was still fast asleep when the

children approached from the river. Wolf gave a bark and Cunval staggered to his feet. He had been dreaming of battles, with dying bodies trampled underfoot by horses, and with blood oozing onto the grass from hideous wounds. He had clearly pictured his brother, Cynan, and his bishop, Dyfrig. The warriors from the settlement had been in great danger, all fighting for their lives. He knew that this dream would repeat itself every night until the warriors returned.

Rees could see that Cunval did not look well.

"You're very pale, Cunval. You should sit by the fire. Here, have some hot tea." The rest of the children arrived as Cunval took his mug from the side of the fire.

"Well, yes, I seem to have overslept this morning. I've been stoking up the fire all night, you see." Cunval shook his head and perked up. "Now, the next job is to stack all of the pottery inside the kiln, and your figurines, of course, then we can build up a really hot fire, and it will all be set hard."

After properly stacking each item inside the kiln, Cunval blocked the access, leaving enough gap underneath to allow the hot air to flow up through the kiln and out through the top flue.

"Shall I build the fire up now, Cunval?" Rees could not wait to get the fire roaring.

"Yes, we're all ready. Now, this is the wood for you to use, this smaller stuff. If you come with me, children, we'll go down to the river and collect all the small driftwood while Rees feeds this lot into the fire."

Charging down to the river was the start of the game. After an hour, the fire was roaring away and tremendous heat surged through the top of the flue. Cunval judged that the temperature was now sufficient to have fired the pots, so the fire was raked out and the lower opening sealed. After covering the flue, Cunval said, "That's it; all finished. All we have to do now is leave it to cool for a day or two."

"Oh, no. I thought it was ready. We don't have to wait that long do we, Cunval?" Olwen and the children were clearly disappointed.

"Well, I am sorry, but it needs to cool down gradually, or everything will break up." Cunval shrugged and grimaced. "I've been thinking. Now that we've got some time, I can show you how to make a whistle and a flute, and, if you help me, I can probably make up some wooden toys."

This was a time to keep the children occupied and out of the way of the women. Cunval felt it would be at least a week before there was any news from the east, so the busier the children were, the better all round.

The children shrieked with anticipation. Cunval had become an integral part of their lives and, gradually, he was going to lead them away from their old spirit world and all its ridiculous fears and superstitions.

"We'll need lots of tools, Cunval." This was a chance for Rees to show how important he was when it came to making things. He led the way up to the moor, and the first job was to let out the animals.

"The grass in this corral is grazed right down. Will you lot help me to set up a new corral? We can extend it further along the bank, and then the old one will grow again." The children were not too enthusiastic; it looked like hard work. "I don't mean right now. Perhaps we can do it tomorrow?" The children nodded and looked at each other resignedly.

They all walked down to Cunval's enclosure, and soon they had collected branches of sycamore, elder and spindle wood. The process of sliding the bark off short lengths of sycamore and the hollowing out of the elder sticks was watched with great interest. Cunval had set up his workbench near the high cross and, as they all gathered around, he was glad to see that the children were quite comfortable in his cemetery. They hardly noticed Freid's grave, which was now covered over with grass and was always kept tidy. Rees followed Cunval's guidance and they eventually produced whistles and a flute.

Cunval organised them into a group, with Rees trying to play a tune on the flute and the children whistling in time to each note. Wolf sidled off into the garden and Hawk wandered up to the moor; Cunval hoped the women would be able to stand the noise when the children showed them this new game.

When Cunval had been a young teacher at Caerleon, he had carried on the college tradition of making up puppets and putting on a show for the pupils. This was usually connected with Bible stories and was a good medium for teaching. The younger children decided to go for a walk on the moor and blow their whistles at the skylarks. Now was the time to make up some wooden puppet-heads and give the children a treat. With some dry cleft timber from his store, Cunval was able to make up two passable duck heads; the duck bills clacked together and cloth over the back part of the heads behind the big round eyes formed gloves for Cunval's hands. Rees fell about laughing as Cunval coloured the eyes and practised the movements. Wolf was quite interested in these new additions to the group and snapped playfully at the two ducks.

"If we both go inside the hut, Rees, I'll put a hurdle across the door entrance and, when the children get back, they will see two ducks looking over the hurdle."

Rees thought it would be a good idea to hang one of Cunval's hides over the hurdle, and Cunval outlined a story for them to enact. They would each assume a duck voice. Cunval would operate the puppets from below, Rees would remain out of sight, and pinch his nose to give the appropriate sound effect. They practiced for a while, but Rees was barely able to stop laughing.

Presently, the children arrived back at the enclosure, calling, "Where are you?" Wolf was sitting in the middle of the enclosure, looking at the hut.

"Look," said Olwen. "Somebody's closed off the doorway to the hut. Are you in there, Rees?"

The head of a duck slowly appeared above the hide. It looked both ways, then quacked loudly. This made the children jump and run for the gateway. They then peered around the fencing as the duck moved back and fore above the hide, quacking. When they realised it was Cunval and Rees, the children approached gingerly and sat on the bench, fascinated.

"Quack, quack. my name's Dwolwen. I've lost my little boy. Has anyone seen a little boy duck? Quack, quack." The duck's bill clacked as he spoke.

"No!" shouted the children together.

"Well, his name is Dwees, quack. He keeps wandering off, and I've lost him, quack."   Just then, another duck raised its head above the hide. The children shrieked and pointed, "There he is!"

"Qua-a-a-a-ck, is that you, Dwees?"

"No, I'm not Dwees. My name's Peder. I'm a pigeon, coo, coo." The second duck raised himself up and preened.

"He's not a pigeon," screamed the children.

"Quack, quack. You don't look like a pigeon. You don't talk like a pigeon. Where have you been?"

"I've been swimming on the big pool, coo, coo."

"Quack, pigeons can't swim, quack."

"Coo, I was sitting on a swan, coo."

This knockabout comedy went from strength to strength; the children were in hysterics, and Cunval and Rees improvised between bouts of laughing. Finally, they were both exhausted from their efforts, and the ducks had to go home for supper.

"How about some honey cakes?" Cunval peeked over the hide and then dismantled the props. The children wanted to see the ducks, but Rees insisted that the poor ducks must go home now and might return tomorrow.

"I need some hot milk. How about you, Dwees?" joked Cunval.

"Why yes, Mrs Duck, some hot milk!"

Whilst making up his fire, Cunval was bombarded with questions. Broth and cakes were then served. It was a relief to sit on the bench in the warm sunshine, although the enthusiasm of the children could be a little wearing sometimes.

The afternoon was spent at the shallow pool; the games of swimming, boating and checking the fish-traps were endless sources of fun. Although Cunval's aim was to occupy the children whilst the warriors were away, he also realised that he needed to be constantly occupied himself; the thought of bloody battles in the east was oppressive and worrying for him.

The next day it was arranged that the women would visit the kiln for the grand opening up. Cunval was quietly confident that most of the pottery would survive; in any case, he was prepared for the next batch, and Rees was so looking forward to seeing success with his new-found skill as a potter.

In the evening, Cunval had thought up a joke to play on the children. It had once happened to him as a lad at Caerleon, and he hoped they would not be too frightened. He planned that, when the children arrived next morning at the kiln, he would coax them into the wood, where he would set a trap. During the evening, he looked for a suitable tree where he could climb up to the higher branches and hang a rope of elm bark. He found a suitable oak tree overlooking the pathway that led along the bank below the moor. He then gathered a large quantity of bracken and tied it up into a huge ball. This he tied to the rope and carried up the sloping pathway to another tree, covered with ivy. This made a good hiding place, and the length of rope worked out just right. Cunval now practised releasing the ball of fern and watching it zoom down the path in a large arc and with a loud swishing noise. It then returned along the pathway towards him. This would surely shock the children and make them jump. He practised a few times and quite enjoyed making the final adjustments.

Cunval sang on his way back to the hut, and, after supper he knelt at his cross in the setting sun. Summer was drawing to a close and there was a slight chill in the air. That evening he tried to rationalise the tragic position that the settlement was in and, with deep meditation, he tried to speak with his God, and communicate his thoughts to his brothers in Caerleon. He wondered if they were trying to do the same thing. The nights would be endless until there was news.

chapter 21

Busying himself with the morning chores enabled Cunval to put the night's dreams behind him. His goat, the cattle and sheep, the bees and all the wildlife were blissfully unaware of any drama to the east. God's creatures were an inspiration to him and a constant source of comfort. Walking along the moor with them as they spread out looking for the day's sweetest grazing, he chattered and sang. The season's younger animals were now grown and were out of danger from foxes and wolves. Cunval thought they might be better left out at night to boost their fitness for the coming winter.

However, there was business to attend to; Cunval ran down to his kiln, to check the cooling down process. He slid the top stone partly to one side to allow the hot air to escape, and peered down into the dark interior. All looked well. He hoped that after a few hours he would be able to open up the access fully and delight the women with some new jars and pots. He explained all this to Wolf as he made these preparations, and the old dog, as usual, lay down, with one ear cocked.

There was no sign of the children, but Hawk's barking across at the settlement was telling them it was time for the day's first adventure. Cunval made his way to the hiding place and sat down with his bread, butter and cheese for breakfast.

Before long, the children had called at the enclosure and the corral, and then made their way to the kiln. They wondered whether Cunval was down at the river, and called his name in unison. As they listened for his reply, the loud call of a raven permeated the woods.

"That sounds a bit odd," said Rees. "I think that's Cunval pretending to be a raven." All went quiet again as the children looked around to see where the noise was coming from.

The loud raucous noise once more filled the air. "Over there," pointed Olwen. "Along the pathway. Come on, let's catch him!"

The children charged along the pathway, but came to a stop as a blood-curdling groan echoed through the wood. The next thing they knew, a huge object came hurtling towards them. They didn't have time to assess what on earth it was. They all dived for the edge of the path and finished up sprawled in the undergrowth as the ball of fern swooped down on them with a loud 'whoosh'. Their shrieks had hardly subsided when the ball reached its zenith and came back down the path, to make them duck once again.

"What is it?" shouted Olwen.

This was obviously the work of Cunval. Their mock outrage turned to hysterical laughter as they watched the ball sweep back and forth. Rees was brave enough to try and catch it and slow it up, then they all peered along the pathway for the source of this trickery.

"Let's go!" shouted Rees, leading the gang. They got to the ivy-clad hiding place. "There's nobody here! But look!" The dried-out skull of a long-dead sheep was impaled on a stick driven into the ground, and feathers were sticking out of the eye sockets.

"Ach!" winced Olwen. Just then they heard the sound of singing in the wood and, as it grew louder, Cunval appeared, innocently singing as he walked along the pathway.

"It was you, it was you. You can't scare us, Cunval. You thought we would run away from that fern demon in the sky."

The children pulled at Cunval's sleeves as Olwen scolded him.

"What demon? It couldn't have been me. I've been for a nice morning stroll with my dog and, arghh! What's that?" Cunval knelt in front of the sheep's skull and stared into its long gone eyes. "Do you know, I think this is the work of the evil underground spirits. I bet it was those devils we disturbed down in the badgers' set yesterday."

The children burst out laughing; any notion of earth spirits was now a thing of the past, and Cunval was proud of this demonstration of their commonsense. He turned to look at them with an open mouth and a twinkle in his eye.

"On the other hand, it could have been one of the ancient spirits from the big pool, who swam down river and…"

"No, no, no. We know who it was." Cunval was saved further questioning by the call of the women, who were at the kiln.

"Aha! We must attend to the magic kiln spirits." Cunval raced off down the path with the shrieking children in hot pursuit.

Cunval could sense that the women gathered at the kiln were trying to appear as normal as possible. The empty settlement was, undoubtedly, very unnerving for them.

"Good morning, ladies. Shall we open the kiln?" Cunval was confident, after his earlier inspection, so he took away the top stone covering the flue and started to remove the stonework to the access. Rees was an eager helper, and the children tried to peer inside at their handiwork. As sunlight pierced the top hole, Cunval could see that there had been only a partial collapse on the one side of his pyramid of pots and jars. He squeezed his shoulder and arm inside, carefully removed the top jars and passed them to Rees, who, in turn, whistled with admiration and passed them on to the women.

"They feel all right, Cunval. They're still quite hot." Anhared passed one of the larger pots to Helga, who nodded and praised Cunval for his clever work.

"Now, let me get at the figurines. Here Olwen, what do you think?" Cunval passed out the various animals and birds that the children had made, and they were ecstatic. His own work, a fish, had fired nicely. He flicked at each item with his finger-nails, to produce a ringing sound. "I'm afraid some of the drinking mugs are damaged, but don't worry, children. We can make some more in the next batch."

Cunval had to clear some of the debris from inside the kiln, but, all in all, he was very pleased at this first attempt. The women were also pleased for they could now continue with making their preserves and storing honey.

"Next time, I'll do one more batch of jars and mugs, and I'll try and make some jugs with handles as well. Then,

I'll get to work to make some huge storage jars. I expect the warriors will be glad of them for beer making."

The women looked at the ground; they hoped all the men would return safely. The children studied the mugs with their names on them, but the two smaller boys were unfortunate to have lost their mugs with the breakages. Cunval took a piece of flint and scratched their names on two of the spare mugs.

"There. That will do for now. I'll make you some more in the next batch. Well, I have to say, Rees, I would never have got this far without your help. One day, you'll be able to do the whole job on your own."

Cunval ruffled his hair as Rees stepped proudly onto the stone shelf and folded his arms in triumph. Gwenhaen started to place the pottery in trugs that the women had brought with them.

"We'll visit Fried's grave while we're over here, Cunval. We can collect the pots on the way back to the river. Are there many flowers on the moor?"

"Yes, of course," replied Cunval. "I'll go on ahead and make some refreshment."

"I know where there are some nice flowers." Rees was already taking Gwenhaen's arm and leading her to the pathway through the wood. Cunval winced as he realised that Rees had a trick up his sleeve. He hoped the women would not be too angry and blame an innocent priest. "Follow me, grandma. This way leads on up to the moor."

Everyone followed Rees and Olwen. Rees scuttled ahead up the pathway as the women chatted unsuspectingly. Cunval was already in his enclosure when he heard the screams of the women. The laughter of the children lingered as Cunval stoked his fire and said a little prayer.

By the time the women arrived back, Cunval was prepared. They scolded him for his devious games and his sinful influence on the children. Anhared sat on the bench with her arm around Olwen.

"I don't know how you expect to go to heaven, Cunval. You're much too wicked to be a priest!" Cunval gasped with mock outrage, whilst the children laughed and pointed at Cunval with accusing fingers. "If your bishop thought you were behaving like a child, he would send you off to the mountains, to convert the wild goats."

The other women hooted with laughter; Anhared was by far the most outspoken of the group and always ready for a humorous exchange. Cunval explained the laughter to Helga, who was gradually becoming conversant with the Celtic language. She, in turn, was amused, and insisted that Cunval was much too useful to be sent away. Her pregnancy was now showing; this was indeed a blessing. Celts and Saxons coming together with intermarriage and mutual understanding was a good omen for the future. Helga was glad of a chance to speak with Cunval; she had now accepted her fate, and her loved one was away and in danger. She was turning to Cunval for comfort, and he suddenly realised that his destiny was right here and now. God had prepared him for this moment. Helga was much in need of his ministry. Her dignity and pride had ensured her respect, first, as a captive, now, as a willing wife. After falling in love with Catvael and smoothing his rough edges, she was, as with the other women, a wife and an expectant mother whose spirit transcended any boundaries of nationality and separateness.

Tears came to her eyes as Cunval spoke of destiny and fate.

"I don't pray to Woden any more, Cunval. When Freid came to the settlement, she showed the other women that the Gods were not to be feared and could never harm good people."

The other women seemed to be glad that Helga was talking, for they all needed Cunval in their hour of need. They had come to realise that his way of life was pure and simple; he could harm no one and he was dedicated to the service of his fellow human beings. His freeing of the thief had outraged them initially, but they knew now why he had risked everything and wanted to own nothing.

Cunval knelt in front of Helga and took her hand. He explained as best he could what it meant to be a Christian; he promised to teach her of God if she so wished, and he so wanted to tell her of the Bible and of Jesus. As the tears came into his own eyes, Helga leant forward sobbing; this was the hour of her enlightenment. The other women and the children could feel that this moment was a new point in Helga's life and in their own. Cunval noticed that the shadow of his high cross lay over them all.

Shouts from the pathway signalled the arrival of Henbut and the labourers. They wanted to see the products of the kiln. The emotions of the last few minutes subsided, so Cunval made sure that everyone had some vegetable broth. Olwen took charge, and Cunval ran down to greet the men.

"Henbut, Cam, I'm so glad to see you. Look, the women are with me and they're feeling a bit low, but do come and join us. We're just off to the kiln."

Cunval's enclosure was soon busy with conversation and Olwen, with a stern face, shared the food and raw vegetables.

"Listen, everybody," Cunval said, driven to speak by an inner force, "would you like me to pray for the warriors? I don't know what else I can do to help"

Henbut nodded his approval. Cunval ushered the group around the cross and knelt down, facing east. With hands clasped, he prayed aloud, knowing full well that the congregation would not understand his Latin. He then explained that he had prayed for the deliverance of the men folk and for inner strength to be given to all those at the settlement. These prayers seemed to be appreciated, then, without lingering, Cunval suggested that they all go down to the kiln. The merry chatter of the children returned all adult thoughts to the daily routine and brought some semblance of normality.

"Oh yes, very nice!" Cam was the first to pick up one of the larger mugs. He placed it on his head and did a pirouette. "This will keep the weather off. Now, come on, little ones, I think it's going to rain!"

The mood became jovial and boisterous and the women decided to escape back to the hall. The sun was now hot and the children wanted to swim and play.

"Let us help you with the next batch of clay, Cunval," offered Henbut. "We've done our fair share of work in the barn this morning." Henbut understood that every opportunity to keep the community busy was essential.

The next hour was usefully spent kneading the clay and

spreading it out to dry off. Cam interrupted his chatter to look at the inviting river.

"That's it," he said. "I must have a swim. I'm boiling. Come on, boys!"

With that Cam and the three labourers stripped down to their under garments and charged into the shallow pool. The children shrieked as a mountain of water sprayed into the air from the thrashing limbs of the four big men, none of whom could swim properly.

chapter 22

The next few days and nights passed slowly and Cunval made every effort to keep the community busy. He involved everybody in the pottery process and successfully made some large storage jars, jugs and extra cooking pots. The children helped with the extension to the corral and started to enjoy themselves as the fencing took shape. Rees could sense that Cunval was trying to divert all thoughts away from the Saxon crisis and he became a great help with the children. The women busied themselves with the daily chores and spent each evening on the moor, where their thoughts could be closer to the men folk in the east. When the men were due to return, they would come from the east across the moor, so, at appropriate moments, Cunval ran back and forth to various vantage points, to stare into the distance. Perhaps there would be a rider soon; perhaps even the king's envoy.

Brockvael had hardly been seen since the warriors left; he had taken to riding off upstream, sometimes staying away for the night. He did not say where he was going, and Gwenhaen did not ask. Cunval thought he may be going to his former childhood home at the old Hentlan settlement for solace and contemplation. Early one morning, Cunval saw Brockvael enter the shrine area of the settlement spring. He did not stay long before setting off on his horse, and Cunval tried to imagine what he was saying to his gods.

One thing was sure, the pagan gods could no more influence events than even Cunval's puny prayers; the destiny of Penhal was in God's hands.

Eight nights had passed since the warriors had ridden away, and Cunval lay under his bed-clothes, suffering his usual painful dreams. Sometimes, he would wake up, and his prayers would help him to drift back into a fitful sleep. Just before dawn, Wolf whined softly, which caused Cunval to sit bolt upright. He donned his tunic and his leather over-shoes and ran swiftly from the enclosure, at the same time covering his head and shoulders with his cape. The sun was still well below the horizon and there was a slight drizzle. He did not know what was driving him across the moor, he only knew that he must run towards the eastern sky. There was enough light to see the slippery track-ways and, after a while, Cunval had gained the vantage-point at the end of the moor from which he could look down into the Gwei valley. With Wolf panting beside him, Cunval breathed deeply to regain his composure and peered intently into the gloom below.

As the sun reluctantly tried to rise above the line of hills in the distance, the shadows in the valley diminished to reveal the fields and groves. One of the settlements already had a fire, which shone brightly between the houses. Suddenly, there was a loud shout of alarm, which carried up from the distant settlement. Cunval leaned forward and strained his eyes to see, but the distance was too great to make out anything other than some vague figures and horses. He had an overpowering feeling of foreboding. Surely, this meant that the war band was returning.

A short while later, Cunval saw a line of horses moving

across the fields towards the moor. There appeared to be seven horses; Cunval tried to count them as the grey light improved. They soon blended into the tree-line and would be lost to sight until the track-way brought them up through the bracken and onto the moor. Cunval clasped his hands in front of his mouth and prayed; the wait was interminable.

There was no sound. Even the birds were silent on this dull, wet morning. The sky to the east had cleared a little, and weak sunshine lit up the greenness of the summer bracken; and then, suddenly, bowed heads appeared above the foliage lining the track-way. Cunval could see Arteg in front, then, one by one, other warriors appeared: Blethyn, Docco, Howel and Hewyn.

They looked exhausted and bloodied, and their horses were near collapse. Cunval was not prepared for what he saw next. The last three horses had human corpses strapped across the saddles. He howled in sheer anguish. This could not be true; surely it was all a dream. The men looked up at the sound of Cunval's cries, but they did not falter in their determined progress. They did not look at Cunval as they passed, for this was the first stage of a funeral procession.

Wolf whined softly and Cunval realised that none of the dogs that had set off with the warriors had returned. Cunval sank heavily to his knees, hardly daring to look up. He was quite familiar with the presence of the dead, but this was somehow different; men killed in battle were part of a human catastrophe, vibrant life wiped from the face of the earth. The corpses had been wrapped in hides, but Cunval knew the horses. Catvael's stallion showed cut-marks and dried blood. On the second horse, Durwit's long hair hung partly exposed below the wrapping, and the third horse carried a lifeless young Maervun, not yet seventeen. Cunval prayed feverishly. He felt so insignificant in the midst of this tragedy, yet he knew that he must show strength. His bishop and his brethren would expect it of him and his new community would crave it.

The procession proceeded slowly across the moor, with Arteg leading the way and Cunval, with bowed head, following the last horse. When, after an eternity, they started to come down to Cunval's enclosure, Arteg called a halt and motioned to Cunval to come forward.

"We will rest here for a short while and drink from your spring. I want you to run on down to Penhal and speak to Brockvael. Tell him the bad news. At this moment, I just can't bear to face the families. We've been travelling since yesterday morning."

"Yes, sire, of course. I'm so sorry. I just can't believe it." Cunval was aware of the other warriors looking upon him as their messenger. They needed him, and he was glad that he was on hand.

Running down the slippery pathway caused Cunval to fall and tumble. Near the bridge, he ran straight into the shallow part of the river, wading and shouting at the same time. Henbut was the first to appear and he helped Cunval up onto the bank.

"Henbut," gasped Cunval. "Tragedy. Catvael is dead, and young Maervun, and Durwit. The warriors are on the way down. I must tell Brockvael."

Henbut moaned and grimaced. He could well remember the occasion when Catvael's older brother was killed, six years earlier; the family had never really got over it. He led Cunval across the field.

Brockvael and Gwenhaen were rushing to the gateway as if they had already sensed the dreaded homecoming. Cunval knelt before them and tried to blurt out the bad news. Henbut helped him to explain. The words were clipped and jumbled and Cunval wept uncontrollably. Brockvael stiffened and stared into the distance. He had been prepared for the worst. He knew Catvael would lead in the fray, and he knew that the leader was always the prime target. No doubt, Durwit had tried to protect him, but they had both fallen.

"Tell Arteg to come here, priest."

Brockvael then took his weeping Gwenhaen towards the spring and the shrine. Henbut strode into the settlement and Cunval, wiping tears from his face, raced back across the river. The warriors had already started down the pathway on foot, leading their tired horses. Cunval waved them on and once more waded into the river to stand on the bank. Howls and screams came from the waking settlement; this was the worst day in Cunval's young life.

The whole community stood weeping near the gateway as the horses entered the water and struggled up the bank to the field. The children clung tightly to the stricken women. Arteg sought Brockvael's narrowed eyes, and led Catvael's horse to him. At the same time, the two younger wives with their children rushed to their exhausted warrior husbands.

Cunval went to Anhared, who had already experienced this saddest of scenes, and helped to comfort Rees and Olwen. Hardly anyone spoke; they were too shocked. Brockvael walked to his shrine at the spring, but Arteg did not follow. Gwenhaen rested her hand on the body of her son and sobbed while Cunval prayed.

Brockvael re-appeared after a few minutes and motioned the procession to the gateway of Penhal. The warriors lifted the bodies of their fallen comrades from their horses and into the house of the dead. The labourers unsaddled all the horses and, after treating their wounds, turned them into the now silent field.

It was left to the older members of Penhal to prepare the bodies for lying in state, and soon the whole community had gone into their respective houses. The warriors would need much rest. Cunval turned sadly to the river and found Wolf on the far bank, lying quietly on the pathway. Could he sense the loss? He slowly followed Cunval to his hut.

At his cross, Cunval collapsed on the grass; he was too weary to kneel. His thoughts now were for his brother Cynan. Was the battle a victory for the king? The warriors of Penhal did not know of Cunval's brother. There was, possibly, some news at Abermenei, and Cunval wondered if he dare leave the settlement to go there. There was not much that he could do, and the cremation of the three heroes would probably be carried out the next morning. It could be that Brockvael would not want to see Cunval before then.

Realising that he was very thirsty, Cunval drank the last of his milk and ate a little cheese. He would go to Henbut and ask his advice. Shutting Wolf in the enclosure and leaving him bread, cheese and a much-gnawed bone, Cunval set off with his staff for the bridge. Skirting around the settlement enclosure, he found Henbut and Mair milking the cows.

"It's a sad day, Cunval. It was a terrible shock to the

community. There's not much you can do here, yourself. The cremations will be tomorrow morning."

Henbut and Mair were clearly upset, and Cunval was hesitant to mention his proposal to go to Abermenei.

"I would very much like to seek news of my brother at Abermenei, Henbut. Pedur would surely have some information. Do you think it appropriate for me to go there and be back tonight?"

"I see no reason why not. Let me go and see Brockvael. He may have a message for Pedur."

Henbut knew how to handle Brockvael and he felt this might be a good chance to offer him some solace at such a difficult time. It may be that Pedur would have some news for him; after all, Brockvael and Pedur were old warriors themselves and had known sad times before.

Cunval helped Mair with the milking. There was an eerie silence over the settlement, and Mair said that the people would remain in their houses for the day and night. Henbut returned and brought news that gave Cunval a purpose for his errand.

"It seems that there was a great victory, Cunval. Brockvael wants you to tell Pedur that he will be visiting in two days time, and he asks you to bring back any news that you can. Cam will go to Blaeno."

Cunval was to take the donkey with him, to speed his journey, and Brockvael's orders were that, on his return, he should report to Henbut with as much detail as possible. He knew that he must also go up to Blaeno, as soon as circumstances permitted, to offer his commiserations to the families there.

"Brockvael spoke to me of the battle. Apparently, after

the enemy were routed, Catvael and Maervun charged into some woods after the Saxons, and they were followed by Durwit. Arteg has been telling him that they were ambushed by Saxon dwarfs, who leapt out of the trees and stabbed them to death. Durwit slew two of the dwarfs but, when Arteg caught up, the three warriors were all dead. It appears that Catvael was much too headstrong and he should have waited until they were all together."

Cunval hung his head in sorrow. He could not criticise the warriors in any way. They were doing what they fervently believed was right, and they were defending their land and their kinfolk. It was not for Cunval to try and fathom the ways of the world. He knew that he could never consider harming another human being; he was weak and incompetent.

"I'll get the mule and be off," said Cunval, "and I'll be back with you before dark." Striding past the west gateway he was startled by a distraught Helga.

"I heard that you were going to Abermenei, Cunval. I just wanted to see you. I can't believe Catvael is dead. Will you pray for his soul? Do you think he will go to heaven, Cunval?" Helga wept and Cunval felt so sorry for her. She hugged her shawl tightly around her body. Her eyes were red-rimmed.

"Yes, Helga. Catvael had good intentions. He gave his life for the protection of his family. He is as much a Christian martyr, in essence, as any of God's other martyrs. I will pray for him, Helga, and you can too. Just ask God to look after him. He will hear you, don't worry."

For a moment, Helga leaned against Cunval's chest, and, in response, Cunval hugged her and patted her back. He hoped that he was truly able to share her grief and anguish.

"Thank you, Cunval," she whispered and returned to her darkened room.

That moment lingered with Cunval as he rode downstream to Abermenei. His congregation was expanding in a most mysterious way. Helga had become a Christian and would respond willingly to further religious instruction. God was indeed helping him in his mission to Penhal, but he would have to be strong.

Chapter 23

Cunval followed the right-hand bank downstream for much of the way. The fields, heath and open country were better suited to the mule, and there was no time to lose. A short rest for the mule as they crossed the river gave Cunval a chance to reflect. He must, of course, report to Pedur, and give Brockvael's message; then, after carefully absorbing any messages he was to carry back with him and learning more of the tragic events of Abermenei, he would enquire about Cynan. This part he dreaded. In any event, a visit to his colleague, Tidiog, would still leave him ample time for the return journey.

The day had brightened up and, shortly after noon, the children, led by young Conmael, ran from Abermenei to greet him. They were very excited about the news of the great victory at Corinium, but had not been told of the losses of Penhal. Cunval listened carefully as Conmael related events as he knew them.

Cynvarch, the king's envoy, had passed through Abermenei late the previous night, to give news of the victory and, with a fresh horse, had galloped on to Caerleon. Another rider had been dispatched to visit Black Rock and the settlements in the south. There appeared to have been losses from each settlement, and it was imperative that the families were informed as soon as possible.

The war band from Abermenei had suffered two deaths,

both young men who had not been fathers; a loss that did not seem to affect the children unduly. Cunval spoke with Conmael as the rest of the gang ran on to the town.

"I have some bad news, Conmael. Rees' uncle, Catvael, was killed in the battle."

Conmael seemed to have grown up since Cunval had last seen him, but he was downcast when he learned that his new friend, Rees, had now lost both his father and his uncle. "Another young man, Maervun, was also killed, and Durwit as well." Cunval realised that speaking of Durwit did not adversely affect him as much as previously. "The settlement at Penhal is very upset, as you can imagine. The funerals will be tomorrow morning."

"Will their souls go to heaven, Cunval?" This was not a question Cunval had expected, and did not really want to address in the case of Durwit.

"There is conflict in my heart, Conmael. Catvael and Maervun will go to heaven, I'm sure, because they were good people at heart, but I cannot answer your question with regard to Durwit. He died fighting for his kinfolk and not for his gods, but, forgive me Conmael, I just don't know what to say about him."

"Why don't you ask God?"

"Well, I can pray to God, and ask him to look after their souls, but no one can actually speak with God."

Children could always ask such direct questions. Cunval was glad when they arrived at Pedur's house. Pedur and his wife, Elise, were both pleased to see Cunval and he was, by now, most glad of the refreshment offered. Everybody in the town was busy.

"King Myric and his army are due to pass through from

Caer Gloy this afternoon, Cunval. The names of the dead have been collected and the king's messengers dispatched to all the various settlements. We have many fires burning, the women are preparing food for the army, and we've had to kill every spare lamb, pig and chicken. How are Brockvael and Gwenhaen?" Pedur, in his description of the losses sustained by the warriors, had almost answered Cunval's concern for his brother, Cynan. He would, nevertheless, have to ask the question.

"They are very upset, Pedur. The whole of Penhal is in mourning, and the funeral is tomorrow. Brockvael says he and his wife will visit you in two days' time. Sire, before we speak further, can I ask you if Cynvarch said anything of my brother, Cynan? He is one of the king's captains." Cunval searched Pedur's eyes for any flicker of recognition.

"No, I'm sure Cynvarch would have told me if such a man had perished, or been badly wounded. He had carefully written down a list of names and that is not one I recall."

Cunval heaved a sigh of relief and hoped Cynan would arrive with the king later. "Well, sire, I am, of course, instructed to tell you all the news of Penhal."

Pedur and his wife leaned forward. "There is, thankfully, some good news that I can start with," he began. "It concerns the Saxon woman that Catvael fell in love with." Elise gasped and clasped her hands. "She is a most beautiful woman and has become a Christian." Pedur raised his eyes to the ceiling with a resigned sigh.

"Anyway, I think she is going to have Catvael's child." Cunval sat back with a satisfied expression, and Elise shrieked with delight.

"I do believe it must be the work of God, sire."

Pedur groaned. Elise wanted to know all about Helga, and Pedur waited patiently for the rest of the news. It took almost an hour for Cunval to detail the events since his last visit with Rees, especially his enthusiastic account of the new pottery kiln, and, then, after carefully taking in the news of Abermenei to bring back to Penhal, he set off for Tidiog's hut. The children accompanied Cunval for they were hoping King Myric and his army would arrive soon. This was to be a great honour, for they had never seen the king, or such a large host. Tidiog was working on the riverbank and he ran to greet Cunval.

"I'm so sorry to hear of your terrible losses at Penhal, Cunval. The families must be grief-stricken. We have lost two young men from Abermenei, one was a Christian, you know." The two young priests embraced; their religion was being put to the test, and they were both expected to show fortitude and leadership in this crisis. They were able to draw strength from each other and were soon exchanging thoughts and news.

The party made for the cemetery, where Cunval was shown Tidiog's new chapel for the dead. It was made of stone, to a beehive shape, and had a sturdy wooden door. Tidiog had built this small chapel throughout the summer months.

Milk and cakes were given to the children, in order to cut short their boisterous war games, and everybody settled down in Tidiog's hut. They had hardly resumed their conversation when the sound of a galloping horse thundered past and on to Abermenei. The children dashed out to see, and it soon became obvious from the distant sounds, that the king's army was on the way.

The two priests and the children watched in awe as the huge army approached. King Myric, on a magnificent stallion, led the way, dressed in regal flowing robes, his battle armour temporarily discarded. Many of the soldiers were wounded and they were all tired from their exhausting battle and long journey.

The king stared benignly down at the two priests, as he approached; Cunval knew he was almost a Christian, but there had been some doubts at the monastery when, periodically, so-called criminals had been executed at the old Caerleon amphitheatre. King Myric brought his steed to a halt and beckoned to the children. He leaned forward and clutched their hands; Cunval could see that, wherever the king went, he ensured that he would command huge respect from his close contact with the people.

Cunval searched the faces of the mounted soldiers, looking for any sign of Cynan. The tall, wounded soldier behind the king, who was slumped in his saddle, spoke with a rasping voice.

"Sire, these men are Tidiog and Cunval. Cunval is the new priest of Penhal."

Cunval's hair at the nape of his neck stood on end when he recognised the voice, and he dashed forward. The soldier's head was swathed in a bloodied bandage. He smiled down at Cunval as both his hands were grabbed and squeezed. Cunval had not recognised his own wounded brother.

"Cunval," a large hand rested on Cunval's shoulder, "take Cynan into your church and tend his wounds. He is my very best captain and must be expertly cared for. Oh, and tell Brockvael to join me at Caerleon on the first Sunday in

October, when there will be celebrations."

The king had spoken directly to Cunval, then he turned to an officer, to give instructions, and he pointed at Tidiog's high cross. At the same time, Cynan's own aide dismounted and led his captain's horse into the cemetery, with Cunval still clutching his wounded brother's hands and weeping unashamedly. As Cynan was helped from his horse and led into the hut, the army moved on. They were to rest only for a short while at Abermenei before pushing on, for the king wanted to reach Caerleon before nightfall.

Tidiog heated water and set out his various ointments for Cunval to try to ease his brother's pain. Cunval rocked Cynan in his arms.

"I'm so glad you're safe, dear Cynan. Was it really terrible?"

"Yes, my little brother. There were many, many dead, but Corinium is now safe. The Saxons will be pushed back to the coast for a long time."

Tidiog motioned to his cauldron.

"I'm preparing some salmon stew, Cynan. Are you hungry? I've got plenty of bread and cheese, if you prefer."

Cynan burst out laughing as he looked at the serious faces of his two carers. "I'm so glad to be back. Do you know, I confess that I'm getting too old for battle? I should never have been so slow and got this cut to my head. Now, I need rest."

Cynan had been hanging on grimly to try to complete the journey, and now that he had stopped at Abermenei, he was ready to collapse with fatigue. Cunval removed the bandages to Cynan's head-wound, to reveal a deep cut where a slashing sword had exposed his scalp. A balm had been smothered over the matted hair and dried blood, to try to prevent infection; this did not upset the two young priests, who worked feverishly to clear and wash the wound. They applied new dressings to a now unconscious Cynan and, after stitching the gash together with animal gut dipped in boiling water, they laid him back to sleep and covered him in warm hides.

"We must pray, Cunval. He is strong and I'm sure the wound will heal but he needs to stay here, for a few days at least."

The steady flow of cavalry riding past the cemetery had given way to the hubbub of the foot soldiers. A shout caused the priests to go outside, where a soldier was holding two horses draped with two bundled corpses. Other horses carried wounded soldiers, and many more bore corpses; each horse was led sternly by a foot soldier.

"Here priests. Here are the two casualties of Abermenei. The king asked me to pass them over to you."

The senior soldier helped the priests to lay the bodies in the new stone chapel. He then motioned to another limping foot soldier to mount one of the spare horses. After helping him up, he himself mounted, and joined the rear of the column. There must have been fifty dead being returned to their families. The two priests felt so helpless and saddened.

The children had followed the king down to Abermenei, so, after checking that Cynan was comfortable, the priests prepared the two bodies in the mortuary. They were young men, still under twenty, younger even than the priests were, and soon to leave no trace on this earth. Cunval wondered about Helga and her baby. He felt that every brave young soldier should have known the joy of fatherhood before going off to battle.

The priests prayed at the high cross. The quietness of the cemetery now felt strange after all the noise and bustle of the previous hour.

"Cunval, you must return quickly to Penhal. You have so much to report to Brockvael, and I'm sure he will let you return here tomorrow, after the cremation. Now, don't worry, Cynan will be safe here with me. I won't leave him for a moment. He needs lots of sleep and I'll make sure he eats later."

Cunval was reluctant to leave Cynan, even for the night, but Tidiog took charge of the situation and sent his friend on down to Abermenei.

The king's men and Pedur had been celebrating, and every drop of ale and cider had been consumed by the thirsty soldiers. Most of the army had pushed on to Caerleon, whilst a large contingent had left to follow the Gwei southwards. There would be much grieving tonight as the various families were reunited with their dead heroes. Cunval took his leave of Pedur and, by late afternoon, the children were accompanying Cunval on the first part of his return journey.

Sometimes riding the mule, sometimes running on foot, he reached Penhal by late evening and reported to Henbut. He was taken directly to the hall, where everybody had collected to hear the news of Abermenei. Brockvael was seated near the fire with his warriors and he motioned for Cunval to sit on a bench facing him. Cunval was still breathless from his journey, but a pensive Brockvael nodded and leaned forward as Cunval described the magnificent arrival of the king, the number of dead and wounded, and the news from Pedur. Talking non-stop to an attentive audience, Cunval was only interrupted occasionally by Brockvael, who asked him to repeat various points. There was an approving grunt as Cunval related the king's request for Brockvael to visit Caerleon in October.

"Give him food and milk, Gwenhaen." Brockvael lay back in his seat and stared at the gloom of the ceiling. "You've done a good job, priest. This is a sad day, but we all know what Catvael would say if he were with us now. He would say, 'Do not weep for me, Penhal. I will be watching over you!' Is that correct, Arteg?"

"Yes, sire." Arteg was deeply saddened at the loss of his good friend. Cunval looked around as quiet conversation began to loosen the tense atmosphere. He noticed, in the flickering firelight, Helga standing near her doorway, and he smiled sensitively at her. This was the first time he had been allowed into the hall since the unfortunate incident with Freid, and now he was the centre of attention. God certainly worked in mysterious ways.

"Sire, my brother, Cynan, was badly wounded in the battle and he is recovering at Abermenei. May I return later tomorrow and care for him?" Brockvael looked surprised, but nodded his approval.

chapter 24

The early morning weather had not improved, when Cunval stirred and looked out of his hut door. Wolf was lying by the enclosure gateway, as if on guard and, after a small meal, Cunval went to the corral and quickly carried out his morning chores.

"Do you know, Wolf, I slept so well last night and I can't remember even having one dream? In fact, I feel quite guilty. I should have been having nightmares, after the events of yesterday. Perhaps my brain is suffering from shock." Cunval carried on talking to Wolf as they strode down the path to the bridge.

Henbut and the labourers had prepared a huge funeral pyre the day before and now had the task of being bearers. Cunval decided to wait at the bridge; he did not want to offend Brockvael by appearing to be too familiar. He reflected on the lives of the three dead men. Had they lived, the future of Penhal would have been very predictable. Now, there was a strange vacuum. In a few weeks' time, a new order would emerge, with the settlement looking up to Arteg for inspiration and protection. Brockvael, through age, was no longer a warrior and, without his son, Catvael, and Durwit, his shaman, his authority might well diminish, especially if he was consistently drunk and abusive.

Cynan was in good hands at Abermenei, and a few days of care would ensure that he did not get an infection. With good food, and, of course, plenty of meat, Cynan would regain his strength. Cunval hoped he would stay in the area for a while; as a captain of the king, Cynan had great authority and respect and was free to make his own decisions.

Movement near the north gate told Cunval that the funeral was imminent. He crossed the bridge and took up position at a discreet distance; this was, after all, a pagan cremation and his only real duty was to pray for the souls of the dead warriors. Brockvael and Gwenhaen shuffled from the gateway, flanking a weeping Helga. They stood to one side and waited for the procession to begin. This grouping of the three mourners was very authentic in its way; a Saxon woman, bearing a Celtic child, had been fully accepted by the grandparents. This symbolised an unprecedented coming-together of two nations, and in a remote settlement with a new priest. Indeed, Christianity was pushing its way gently into this pagan enclave.

Arteg and Henbut led the way, bearing the body of Catvael on long poles held at shoulder height. Catvael's ashen face was now exposed, and he was grandly dressed in his warrior's attire. Even after witnessing many funerals at Caerleon, Cunval felt most distressed at the sight of Catvael's mortal remains. The four labourers followed close behind with the bodies of Durwit and Maervun, and then came the women and children, accompanied by the older folk. There was a moment of surprise for Cunval when he recognised Mark and his wife from Blaeno. Maervun was Mark's nephew, and Cunval had forgotten that Cam had hurried to Blaeno to inform Maervun's family of the sad news. They had obviously all ridden down river early that morning, and now Mark's sister and her husband followed them. Mark and his wife would be thinking about the loss of their own son, six years earlier.

Cunval took the arm of the elderly Olivia for the short walk across the field, and soon the whole community was spread out in front of the raised platform that formed the centre of the pyre. With the bodies in place, the labourers took long branches of ash and alder with wilted leaves and stacked them in a dense conical shape around the pyre.

Animal fat and dry kindling wood ensured that the fire, once started, soon blazed fiercely. Tears trickled from every eye, including Cunval's; a funeral was the same, no matter what the race or religion. On this occasion there was no service, just quiet contemplation and personal prayers. When the fire started to die down, there was a penetrating emptiness. Cremations were uncompromising.

When the community eventually drifted back towards the settlement, Cunval spoke to Mark and his sister, offering sincere commiserations. They were going to return to Blaeno later that day.

"We would all like to visit Freid's grave, Cunval," said Mark. "She had told us not to come to her funeral, you know, but to visit later, in our own good time."

This was very pleasing for Cunval, for he would be able to show them his enclosure and garden, and the corral. Freid's grave impressed the family; they knew of Christian burials from the cemetery of Hentlan, and Cunval felt that they were all candidates for conversion at a future date. They were able to pay their respects at the graveside and then inspect Cunval's domain.

Mark's sister spoke as they all stood on the moor, looking eastwards. "Would you mind if we stayed on the moor for a while, Cunval? Is this the route that the warriors took when they first set off?"

"Yes, they were all in line and I followed them for a while. They knew that they were in for a tough fight. I could never ever go off like that, myself. I'll see you later."

Cunval took Wolf across the bridge to the now-empty field. He needed to speak to Henbut. At that moment, the children appeared at the gateway and ran to Cunval. Their mothers had suggested that they go for a walk upriver, and then bring the cattle back for milking later. This would be a chance for some return to normality.

Cunval was surprised when Arteg appeared and strode towards him.

"Cunval, I can't stay here. I'm going to Abermenei for a few days, and you can ride on my horse with me. I'll be leaving after noon."

"Why, yes, sire, that's very kind of you. Oh, I can introduce you to my brother, Cynan. He is convalescent at Abermenai. I'm sure that you have much to talk about."

Arteg nodded and turned away. After strolling for a short distance along the riverbank, Rees began to question Cunval; he wanted to know more of the battle, and all about Cynan and his wound. At least, they had not been subdued by the sad events, and Cunval was witness, once more, to the resilience of children. After an hour or so of walking and chatting, the old bond between Cunval and the children remained intact. Rees took charge of the direction they followed and asked the most pertinent questions.

"Are Christians burnt up sometimes? Do the dead Saxons go to another place to join their god Woden? Do dogs and horses have souls?"

Cunval answered as best he could. His thoughts were elsewhere and he was anxious to get to Abermenei. When they drove the cattle back to Penhal, the warriors were standing at the big pool paying their last respects. Just after noon, Cunval suggested that the children and the dogs go up to the moor to play. They could look after Wolf and keep an eye on Cunval's enclosure whilst he was away. Arteg motioned that he was ready to set off, and the warriors helped Cunval onto the large horse, where he was to sit behind Arteg. The ride down-river was most uncomfortable and Cunval had to hang on tightly to Arteg's leather tunic. There was no conversation until the halfway point, where Cunval had crossed with the mule only the day before. Arteg steered his horse into the river while the travelling companions were able stretch their legs on the bank and enjoy a short rest. Arteg leaned against an alder tree, staring down-river.

"I'm not much help to you, Arteg. I only wish there were something I could do. You now have to be stronger than the rest, for they will all be depending on you for guidance."

Arteg turned to look pensively at Cunval. He raised his eyebrows slightly and nodded. Cunval was pleased with this moment of closeness with the new leader; it seemed that Arteg was glad of his moral support. As they were mounting the horse again, Cunval felt he had become a friend to Arteg. He was looking forward to introducing him to Cynan. The rest of the trip was uneventful until the town children, led by Conmael, raced down the river bank of the Gwei to greet them. Cunval slipped off the back of the horse to run towards them in a mock charge.

"Here, Conmael. Do you know Arteg?"

As Arteg rode up, Conmael looked down shyly; he was overawed by the presence of the large mounted warrior. Arteg smiled for the first time and jumped down from his horse. He grabbed Conmael and threw him up into the saddle. The other children gasped as Conmael struggled to sit upright and hold the reins. The horse bucked, scattering the children, and Arteg burst out laughing.

"Well, are you going to be a warrior young man? We need lads like you for training."

"I can shoot arrows," boasted Conmael, "and I go hunting with my father!"

"Excellent," said Arteg, as he led the horse towards Abermenei. Pedur's house was the first call, where they were given some welcome refreshment. Pedur and his wife were pleased to see Arteg, for they had known his parents before their death from the plague at Hentlan, and Arteg had always felt close to them.

"Brockvael will be coming down here tomorrow, Pedur. I hear that you lost two men. Were there many badly wounded?"

The two men spoke of war and victory. Pedur, like Brockvael, had gained much experience as an old warrior. They had fought mostly against pirates in the early days. The Saxons, Scots and Picts had long dispatched large raiding parties to the coast and the estuaries after the Romans had left Britannia.

Elise drew Cunval to one side and said, " Tidiog was hoping that you would be back soon. Pedur insisted that the two funerals would be held this evening. The young warriors were both sons of friends, and he wants the burials to be as soon as possible."

Cunval nodded; this was, indeed, a busy time for all. "How is my brother, Cynan," he asked. "Did Tidiog say?"

"He's fine, Cunval, he's very sore and very annoyed as well, by all accounts." Elise's smile told Cunval all he wanted to know; Cynan was going to be all right.

After arranging for Arteg to stay in Pedur's house for as long as he wished, Elise suggested that Cunval be permitted to visit Tidiog and Cynan.

"Let's go, Cunval," said Arteg brightly, jumping up. His whole demeanour had changed since their arrival at Abermenei; it was obviously a great benefit for Arteg to be away from Penhal for a while. "Well, let's go and meet your brother!" Arteg strode to the door as Cunval struggled to his feet.

The children had taken the horse to the stable and now re-joined Cunval and Arteg as they walked up stream. Conmael was the first to reach Tidiog's enclosure, and soon the priest was running towards Arteg, to clasp his hands. Cunval introduced the warrior.

"I'm so sorry to hear of your terrible loss, Arteg."

"We must all look to the future, priest. We all have our part to play."

Arteg strode into the enclosure and saw Cynan sitting on a bench. He knelt in front of him and stretched out his hands to grip Cynan's shoulders. The two soldiers looked into each other's eyes; there were no words necessary to communicate.

"I hope these two priests are not going to finish you off, Cynan!" The two men laughed heartily; they had never met, but they were comrades in arms.

"You had some bad luck at Penhal, Arteg. There were many losses, but the victory was worth it. The Saxons will be pushed back forever. Tidiog has told me all about Penhal. It sounds like a place worth fighting for!"

Cynan was obviously still in some pain and Cunval inspected his bandaging.

"Stop fussing, please, Cunval, and help me up. I need to sit on the riverbank with Arteg. We have much to discuss." Cynan held out his arms and stood upright, keeping his head slightly raised. "A little walk will help. Strangely, I feel stiff all over. I must be getting old."

Cunval smiled; his brother was only six years older than he was, but fighting in battle was exhausting at any age.

"There's plenty of food, when you're ready," offered Tidiog.

The two soldiers were glad to be alone on the riverbank and they talked quietly as the priests arranged for the funerals. Tidiog led Cunval to a wattle screen near the mortuary. His enclosure was much larger than Cunval's.

"You see, I've dug the grave and it's almost ready, but the first burial is to be the other boy, the pagan. His family want him buried in the old Roman cemetery alongside the roadway; in fact, Pedur asks for all the burials to be there. He doesn't agree with pagan cremations and ceremonies, but, of course, he has no objection to our Christian burials, as long as they're out of sight." The two priests laughed uneasily; in truth, they were almost overwhelmed with the enormity of recent events.

chapter 25

The family of the young pagan warrior had stayed in Tidiog's enclosure for much of the previous night and, as the evening sun began to lengthen the shadows, they returned home, to make their preparations for the burial. The younger brothers and sisters had now realised that they would never see their dear brother again, and this gave the priests an opportunity to offer some comfort.

The community of Abermenei had started to gather at the old Roman cemetery, and friends of the family arrived at the chapel to act as bearers. A horse was found for Cynan, and soon a funeral procession started from Tidiog's gateway. Cunval was amazed at the number of people gathered at the graveside; many had arrived from outlying farms, which swelled the congregation to over a thousand. The two priests stood back as the warriors gathered around to pay their last respects. There was no shaman and no chanting to the gods. As soon as the body was lowered into the grave, and some token weaponry placed beside it, the group of warriors shovelled in the loose soil, to seal their comrade into his final resting place. The leader of Abermenei's war band spoke with Arteg and Cynan, and as the warriors all stepped back, the family laid flowers on the fresh earth.

Pedur took the reins of Cynan's horse and led the second procession, to the Christian cemetery. The whole town followed on, and the priests could hardly believe it when

Tidiog's enclosure became packed shoulder to shoulder, with many more outside, looking over the stone walls. The Christian family took their son from the mortuary, and many hands helped to raise the body for all to see. Tidiog spoke the Christian service in the Roman tongue, which had little meaning for most, but which, at the same time, was inoffensive to the pagans. The white linen shroud was in stark contrast to the previous warrior burial, and there were no grave goods, save a simple copper cross, clipped above the heart. There was little sound except the sobbing of the family and, once again, the burial was soon complete. Pedur turned for the gateway, and Cunval noticed a slight hesitation in his stride as he looked up at the high cross.

The children had been mesmerised by the presence of Cynan and Arteg, and had watched their every move. It was now time for some food, and the children gladly accepted some fish stew, bread, cheese and butter. There was abundant milk, but, when Cynan asked for some ale, he was immediately berated by Cunval, much to everyone's amusement; a mere priest was admonishing a warrior and giving strict orders for him to drink his milk.

Arteg was still laughing as he rose from the bench and table.

"I'm leaving this place before these Christians get their hooks into me. I'd better call again in the morning, Cynan, just to make sure you're still alive." Arteg winked at Cynan. "I think I'll seek a little entertainment in the town, and perhaps I can fix a little something up for you, comrade!"

Cynan waved weakly as Arteg left with the children; he knew that the only way to improve his health was to eat and sleep. Nevertheless, the thought of spending day after day with the two priests was a bit daunting.

"We must tell Tidiog all about our family home, Cynan," said Cunval keenly. "Remember that lovely stream where you taught me to fish?"

Cynan groaned and started to rise. He pretended to faint, and was helped to his bed. Cunval and Tidiog talked until well into the night, then they walked in the moonlight along the riverbank, and prayed at the new grave. The morning sun was well up when Cynan called for some hot stew. He appeared to be much brighter, but winced when Cunval inspected his wound, and then lovingly put his arms around his brother's neck to give him a hug.

"You can bathe in the river today," offered Tidiog, "as long as you're careful not to slip." Cynan nodded and sighed as he realised that this would help to relieve the boredom; his main concern was to get well enough to be able to gallop off to Caerleon.

After breakfast, Tidiog eagerly cleaned his cauldron and the wooden platters, and his chalice and cross. Cunval fetched Tidiog's goat and tethered it where it could graze the grass of the enclosure. Cynan, meanwhile, laid out his warrior's possessions and started to clean and polish them. His sword gleamed in the sunlight, and his wicked-looking dagger caused the priests to avert their eyes. Leather belts and brass buckles were laid out on the grass next to Tidiog's chalice and cross, but Cynan was unaware of the anomaly. The priests sang to themselves happily, and Cynan unconsciously hummed, his thoughts far away. Tidiog's garden occupied the rest of the morning.

The sun grew hot and Cynan agreed to bathe with the priests. With the three men in their undergarments trying not to slip down the bank, their laughter echoed along the valley.

They waded into the shallow water, Cynan supported by his two helpers, until they were all waist-deep in the cool water.

"Now lie back, Cynan, and let the water soothe you." Cunval took over and his older brother protested, but to no avail.

Cynan was much larger than Cunval and very muscular from years of tough training. He hissed a little as the priests removed the dressing from his head and inspected the wound. It was red raw but starting to heal, and the priests decided to wash Cynan's hair with clay and river mud. This they did gently enough, and then Cynan had to suffer the indignity of being covered from head to foot in mud. Cunval insisted that this was part of the cleaning and healing process, and the two priests deftly rubbed the soft mud over Cynan's body.

Singing merrily together and busy in their duties, they only became aware of spectators with the sound of a nervous cough. As the three bathers looked upward, Brockvael, Gwenhaen and Arteg stood on the bank, staring down at them. Arteg was having difficulty containing his mirth, but Brockvael had not expected to see the king's captain in such a pose. He quickly escorted Gwenhaen on to the enclosure, leaving Arteg to tease Cynan mercilessly.

"I'm so pleased to see you," said Cunval, as he dashed into the enclosure to get Cynan's clothes. Brockvael kept a straight face as Gwenhaen handed the bundle of garments to Cunval. "We'll be back shortly," shouted Cunval, as he disappeared again, deftly holding up his own slipping undergarment.

When Cynan led the party from the riverbank into the enclosure, Arteg took over the introductions. Brockvael had known many warriors, and Cynan impressed him very much. Gwenhaen was anxious to see his wound. She could not disguise an intake of breath, and helped to apply ointments and re-dress the wound.

Brockvael was sober and of pleasant disposition.

"That journey on horseback was enough for one day," he complained. "We thought we would walk with Pedur to the Roman cemetery and then come on here to pay our respects to the other dead boy."

They all walked over to the new grave, and Cunval thought that Gwenhaen may have acquired greater influence over her husband; she was now an essential companion to Brockvael. The priests suggested refreshment. As Cunval combed what was showing of Cynan's wet hair, Tidiog handed around mugs of hot, thin broth. Benches were arranged, and Cynan commiserated with Brockvael on his recent loss. He had not known Catvael but had heard of his bravery, and the warriors talked further of war. Tidiog thought it prudent, meanwhile, to show Gwenhaen his garden.

When they returned, Gwenhaen had an announcement.

"There is a feast at Pedur's house tonight and he would be pleased if you all came. Are you well enough to travel, Cynan?"

"I'll bring a horse," said Arteg. "I need to show Cynan some of the town, and introduce him to the various families."

"Well that was all very civilised," said Tidiog, when the

visitors had departed. "I thought Brockvael was supposed to be a tyrant."

Cunval smiled and raised his eyebrows. "He's quite a different person since his terrible loss. I suspect he's suffering from shock and grief at the moment." He turned to Cynan. "Now, dear brother, I've been thinking. I'm going to make you a leather skull cap. I'm sure it will be more comfortable. Tidiog, do you have some light leather and twine?"

Cynan decided to go for a nap and leave the priests to their little games. He knew he would feel better after some sleep, and then he could look forward to some wine and ale later. The thought of fresh roasted meat gave him a contented smile as he lay his head back on the heaped woollen cushions.

Arteg arrived well before sunset, with the children in tow, and soon Cynan was astride the horse, looking very pleased with life.

"I must say, Cynan, your new leather skullcap looks very distinguished. It will no doubt be most attractive to the ladies."

Cynan growled at Arteg and spurred the horse. The priests and the children followed on, forming yet another procession along the old Roman road. The town was bustling again. Mourning for the dead now over, it was time to celebrate the victory. Cunval and Tidiog had arranged to visit the Christian families who lived in the town, but first they must attend the banquet. Pedur's Great Hall in the high Roman bath-house had been decorated with greenery and flowers. Oil lamps were already alight, showing up the weapons that adorned the walls of the large hall. Benches and tables were arranged around the perimeter, and in the centre was a huge table with bread, cheeses, butter and fruit. Beef, lamb, pork and chicken were roasting in the recess that had once been a doorway and now had a chimney with hanging irons and spits. There was much ale, freshly made, and more wine had been rushed from Caerleon, by the order of the king.

Cunval whispered to Tidiog as they gazed about them, "I've seen these banquets in Caerleon. I dare say this will go on all night. I hope we can escape, later!" The priests chuckled and selected some seating in the shadows.

The children of the town were charged with serving the guests, and Conmael and his younger brother came to the priests with wine and ale. The hall was soon full and drinks were rushed to the tables as warriors, labourers and old folk shouted for more. There was no class distinction at Celtic banquets; the gods were forgotten and the warriors teased the older ladies. Children were hoisted aloft, and boisterously thrown shrieking into the air. As the hubbub grew louder, Pedur entered with his wife, followed by the main guests, Brockvael and Gwenhaen. The gathering turned toward him, shouting, "Hail, Pedur!" He was the official host and the most important man in the town. He took a goblet and drank red wine with gusto.

As the meat was carved and handed around, Cunval quietly asked Conmael for some bread and cheese, but Tidiog was an eater of meat, when the chance arose, and he soon tackled a thick slice of pink beef.

"This beef is delicious, Cunval; are you sure you won't try a little morsel?" Tidiog was sympathetic.

"I did try it once," replied Cunval, "but I just couldn't keep it down. I know it's good for you, but, really, I'm quite happy with all this other food."

Tidiog had been sipping his wine with relish. "This wine is good. I think we should be careful not to drink too much."

Cunval hiccupped and remembered the incident at Penhal when the warriors had got him drunk; he was certainly going to be careful, no matter how much goodness was in the wine. For a moment his thoughts turned to Catvael. "Poor Catvael," he murmured.

It was good to see the community so happy. Many of the townspeople had to squeeze into adjacent rooms, and Cunval realised that Pedur must have organised a huge number of people to make the ale and slaughter the animals for this important occasion. Brockvael was a true guest of honour and, as the mead took hold, he started to thump the table and boast of past battles, to impress the younger warriors. Despite Gwenhaen's attempt at holding him back, Brockvael grabbed a sword from the wall and started to slash at an imaginary foe. As the adjoining guests ducked under the table, the nearest warriors wrestled with the laughing, drunken gladiator. This was the first time that Cunval had seen Brockvael laughing.

As the evening grew even more boisterous, the ladies began to slip away to a quieter room. Cunval noticed, with some satisfaction, that Cynan was eating and drinking with ease. He had rested his head against a shelf behind his bench, to help keep his neck relaxed.

An old gentleman next to Tidiog started to cough and needed to be helped from the hall. "This is a good excuse for us to go visiting," whispered Cunval. "Shall we shuffle through the crowd?"

Nobody took any notice of the priests, and several older

people also took advantage of the opportunity to make a furtive exit. The fresh air was welcome as they helped the old man to his house. Tidiog knew the way to the homes of the two bereaved families and they were agreeably surprised to find that Pedur had sent roasted meat to them, knowing that they would not be expected at the hall.

Only some of the houses of the town had lights showing and, luckily, a full moon helped the priests to find their way. They spent an hour with the families, and others had gathered at the Christian house, so Tidiog was able to hold a service. Then, on their way back to the east gate, they came to a house exuding signs of riotous merry-making.

"It seems that some people are holding their own party, Tidiog. I bet they will have sore heads in the morning." The priests laughed knowingly, but then Cunval stopped and listened at the door.

"Do you know, I think that's Cynan's laughter? I'm sure that's him. For goodness sake, I hope he's not going to get drunk and hurt his wound."

Cunval leaned forward and knocked at the door. The merrymaking continued, so Cunval gently pushed at the door and it swung open. He had not expected to be confronted with such debauchery; two partly dressed warriors were on a huge bed with three naked, shrieking girls. As the two priests stood open-mouthed in the doorway, Arteg and Cynan swung around to confront the intruders. Then, they looked at each other and burst out laughing.

"Grab them, girls. The priests want to join in!"

Arteg's command was immediately seized upon by the giggling girls, who grabbed Cunval and Tidiog by the arms and pulled them protesting inside. The warriors threw the two priests onto the bed and held them down, while the girls pulled at the priests' tunics, causing them to cry out with shocked embarrassment. As the warriors laughed hysterically and winked at the girls, the spindly legs and the undergarments of the priests were exposed to the world. The girls tried to kiss the priests, who squirmed and writhed like eels. They all finished up on the floor, tangled up in hides and lost sandals, and with the warriors helplessly collapsed on the bed. Tidiog was the first to crawl to the doorway, closely followed by his distressed companion. Cunval then stood defiantly in the doorway, hands on hips.

"You two should be ashamed of yourselves; you're leading these poor girls astray."

With that, the priests fled from the house, followed by the raucous laughter of the revellers. They ran barefoot along the roadway and into to the safety of their holy enclosure.

chapter 26

After talking late into the night and being sporadically woken by Tidiog's snoring, Cunval rose with a slight headache. His dreams had encompassed the enticing visions of naked girls, and he felt ashamed at the weakness of his male desires. He had also dreamed of a theological argument with Tidiog and his beloved Bishop, over the question of eating meat. He thought it best not to mention his dreams to Tidiog; dreaming was his own personal burden.

"Well," laughed Tidiog as he prepared morning milk, "are you going to excommunicate Arteg and your wicked brother? Their behaviour was quite atrocious. I think I'd better say a little prayer for their souls!"

Cunval realised that Tidiog's teasing was meant to keep the previous night's antics in perspective. Of course, he forgave the warriors, they had been through a very traumatic experience and deserved to forget the horrors of battle for a short while.

"I'm here to lead by example," stated Cunval gravely. "Remember, we must all learn from each other. Now, shall we take a nice walk up the riverbank? We can take some bread and honey for breakfast, and some cheese."

"A good idea, brother Cunval; it will take our minds off the opposite sex."

Tidiog continued with his jesting as the priests left the enclosure and walked up the riverbank towards the bright morning sky. They talked and laughed easily; it was so good to have an understanding companion, Cunval thought. Most priests drifted into a lifelong friendship with a kindred spirit, and Cunval hoped that he and Tidiog would be able to work in the same area forever.

They came across two resting boatmen, who were taking a near-empty barge back up-river after delivering iron ore to Abermenei.

"Good morning," said the priests in unison. It was important to chat with any strangers and give a good impression of the church. Cunval was very interested in the boatmen's work; his upbringing in Caerleon had given him great knowledge of the world of boats and ships, but he was not familiar with the processes of iron making. The boatmen, in turn, were impressed with Cunval's stories of the seagoing ships that traded with Ireland and Brittany.

"Let us share some breakfast with you," suggested Tidiog. "We have more than enough."

The boatmen were glad of the food, and laughed with the priests when a family of swans cautiously swam near them, looking for morsels of bread. A shout from upriver signalled the approach of another vessel and they all watched an expertly punted barge, laden with huge sacks of charcoal, make its way down the centre of the slow-moving river Gwei.

Humorous ribaldries were hurled back and forth as the barge glided past the breakfast party. The priests looked away, and then Cunval jumped to his feet.

"Let us help you to pull your barge," he offered. "We're going up the river-bank, anyway, and more hands will lighten the work."

Cunval used one of the punting poles to push the craft clear of obstacles, and soon they had hauled the barge a good distance. A set of rocks and swirling water was the point where a cottager was obliged to help pull any barges through the rapids and up to the next stretch of calm, deep water. The old man hardly looked up to the task, so Cunval suggested that he brace himself in the barge to push it further into the stream.

"This is more like it," shouted the old man. "Four of you pulling will allow me to live longer."

By noon the priests were exhausted and took their leave. On the leisurely walk back downstream, they reminisced about their time at Caerleon. Given over to the monastery at the age of nine, they had been enrolled into the college of learning, together with the sons of the aristocracy. Cunval, like Madoc and Tidiog before him, had been willingly initiated into the religious life and had striven for ordination. Now, with their own parishes, they felt enriched and enlightened. If nothing else, they were having success in bringing to the rural population a sense of goodness and tolerance, not to mention a knowledge of hygiene.

The children had gathered at the enclosure when they returned, asking for stories.

"Well," offered Tidiog brightly, "shall we take it in turns, Cunval?"

The town children preferred bloodthirsty tales and were more than satisfied with the story of Herod and the slaughter of the babies. Cunval recalled an old Caerleon legend about a headless horseman with a long sword, and exaggerated as much as he dared in order to keep the children wide-eyed. After a while, Gwenhaen arrived and noted the proceedings with some pleasure.

"We are returning to Penhal soon, Cunval. You should come with us. Pedur and Brockvael have agreed for Tidiog to bring the older Abermenei children to visit soon. It will be good for them. Can you arrange that, Tidiog?"

Tidiog and the children were most enthusiastic, and Cunval, and Rees, of course, could show them the whole estate.

"We'll all walk with you to the Menei," offered Conmael.

In the town, the night's carousing had left its mark. Cynan and Arteg were recovering in the Great Hall, with the three girls in close attendance. The priests tried to avoid any eye contact.

"Well, little brother," said Cynan, "you'll be glad to know that I'm recovering, despite your medical attention. I'm going to ride slowly on to Caerleon later. Come here and hug me. I don't know when I'll see you next, but I'll pass on your fondest affections to mother and father, when I see them."

Cunval's eyes were moistening, especially at the mention of his beloved parents. They had last visited him at Caerleon, when it was known that he had been chosen for a mission.

"God bless you," was all he could whisper.

After the farewells, Cunval was once more hoisted onto the back of Arteg's sturdy horse, and soon Tidiog and the children were taking their leave of him at the Menei.

Life at Penhal settled into a new pattern. Brockvael was withdrawn, his younger wife moved into one of the other houses, Gwenhaen gave most of the domestic orders, and Arteg assumed command of the war band. Cunval kept his distance and reported to Henbut each day, to help with repairs, fencing, collecting firewood and tending the animals.

It was now time to gather the last of the nuts and berries and prepare for the wine-making. The orchards were the focus of attention, and any ripening fruit was harvested for making cider, perry and wine. Cunval repaired the cider barrels; it was a good year for apples, and the labourers relished the thought of having fresh cider before the shortest winter day. As autumn approached and rain periodically swelled the river, the salmon began their final mad rush upstream.

"I've got a splendid idea, men!" Cunval called the boys together. "If we can catch some salmon, I can smoke them in our kiln. Well, what do you think?"

Rees thought he could work it out. Normally, fish was smoked in the rafters of the houses above the fires.

"I've been saving all the wood-chips," Cunval explained, "and all we have to do is fillet the fish, hang them up in the kiln and then let the smoke drift up through the top. Got it?"

The boys were not sure of this new idea, but the thought of catching the salmon was dear to their hunting instincts. The community had nets, made by the experts in Caerleon, and there were so many fish on the move that netting them from the pools was not difficult, even for the children. Cunval left the killing to the boys, but was quite adept at filleting the prime, juicy fish. The strips were hung inside the kiln, and Cunval carefully lit a fire in the firebox. When it was sufficiently alight, he spread on wood chips, to give a thick smoke. While the smoke percolated through the top flue, he used his axe to make up more chips, and then damped down the whole fire with clean soil.

Cunval was surprised when the women arrived on the scene with dressed pork and lamb.

"Well, we heard what you lot were doing," smiled Gwenhaen, "so we're going to try some smoked meat."

Cunval stood aside as the women made a bed of twigs inside the kiln and then placed the meat on top.

"Would you like me to tell you all some parables," offered Cunval. "The smoking will take all day, you know."

"What are parables?" asked Olwen.

"Stories of long ago and other lands," replied Cunval. "You see, people are the same everywhere. There are good and bad."

"What about the Saxons?" countered Rees, not realising that Helga was in the company.

"Yes, the Saxons too, Rees. We only hear of the dreaded warriors, and they know no different way of life. But, one day, they will also stop and think of good things."

Helga understood some of the native language and smiled softly at Cunval's words.

The smoking went on for days, and the fire needed constant attention. It was a relaxing time of the year, with no urgency in the farming calendar. The last of the rough hay was being gathered for winter fodder, and fields had been set aside for strip grazing during the winter. There was much open woodland to the east, where the cattle could forage, and find shelter if snow fell.

The warriors had been preparing a deer-run in a valley upstream, which had traditionally been a natural trap for the wild deer. Once herded inside by the horsemen and the dogs, selected animals could be killed for food and the rest set free. The process could be repeated every few weeks, and this year Rees would be part of the hunt. Cunval shuddered at the thought of the gruesome spectacle as the deer were run down and speared.

On returning from one of the upstream trips, with Rees on his own pony, Arteg approached Cunval.

"Henbut tells me you know of Durwit's old cave."

"Yes, sire. It's about a mile upstream, up in the woods. It's a dreadful place."

"I've been thinking, Cunval, that I'd like to see it. Let's go there."

With that, Arteg pulled Cunval up behind him and turned his horse; followed by Rees, they set off. Opposite the point where Cunval judged the cave to be, the horses waded across the now swollen river. Soon they were up in the woods, and Cunval pointed to a mass of dead trees and thick ivy.

"There, sire. I'm sure that's it."

Cunval did not want to enter the cave; once was enough. Arteg and Rees pulled aside some of the undergrowth, and Rees' low whistle told Cunval that the sight of Durwit's lair was a bit of a shock.

"Rees, go on upstream and find the warriors. They have some fire with them. Tell them I need them here."

"Yes, Arteg," said Rees smartly. He jumped on his pony and set off on his first important mission alone.

"Cunval, collect all the dry wood you can. We're going to have a fire."

With that, Arteg started slashing with his sword, and reduced the foliage and low branches from around the cave entrance into a great heap. Cunval ran back and forth with dry wood, but, somehow, burning up Durwit's home and possessions did not give him any pleasure. Although Durwit was no more, Cunval felt guilty for being part of this destruction.

"Now, pile all the smaller wood inside the cave, Cunval, then add the bigger logs, and then the green branches."

As Cunval got closer to the mouth of the cave, the smell from within changed his mind about any feeling of guilt; the sooner the whole thing was afire, the better.

Soon, Rees arrived with the warriors. They carried with them a metal container of hot charcoal. They had taken fire with them up to the valley, where they had killed a deer. Cunval knew it was normal for the hunters to drink the warm blood and to cook the liver and heart of a fresh deer. The carcass was then brought back to the hall.

The warriors looked around the edges of the firewood, peered into the lair, and immediately turned up their noses; it was obvious that Durwit must have left dead animals inside when he went away.

"Start the fire, men, and get some more wood. I think we should have a good burn-up." Arteg jumped onto his horse and left for Penhal, his job done. The fire soon got going and burnt fiercely. The overhanging rock became black with the smoke, and Cunval decided that he would come back next year, to see how the new season's undergrowth had eradicated this place.

Chapter 27

The next two weeks saw Cunval helping with the thatched roofs. There was much repair needed before winter, and the firewood stacks were now so high that Cunval and the children were able to climb up onto the roofs safely.

The time was approaching when Brockvael and Gwenhaen were due to visit the king in Caerleon. This gave Brockvael a sense of importance once more, and dispelled some of his grief.

However, the week before the visit was due, one of the labourers shouted from the Abermenei side of Penhal. His call meant that a rider was approaching, and the sound of hooves caused Cunval and whole clan to stop work. Looking over the palisade from the Hall roof, Cunval could see a white horse charging up to the gate; it was the king's envoy, Cynvarch.

"Oh, no." whispered Cunval, surely this was not going to mean more trouble. It was probably just a courtesy visit, before the gathering at Caerleon.

Brockvael came to the door of the hall, followed by the warriors. Cynvarch strode across the enclosure.

"There is no danger," he stated straight away, "but a Saxon ship was seen going up the estuary. There was only one ship, just a small raiding party, and it looked as if they were in trouble with the tide. All the war bands on the

Gwei have crossed over and are going through the Forest of Danet to the Hafren. The men of Abermenei have already left, so I want your men, Brockvael, to go over to the east farm and cross to the forest there."

Brockvael nodded sternly, and the warriors looked to him for the next move.

"Come inside, Cynvarch. Arteg, you can get the men ready. The women will soon have provisions for you."

Brockvael sat by the fire with Cynvarch and tried to get any further information before the men set off. It was doubtful whether the Saxons presented any danger, and they would be lucky to survive the Hafren estuary, which was treacherous with a high tide running.

Cynvarch was to accompany the war band over the moor to the east farm, and then continue on to Caer Gloy. Within the hour they were all ready to cross the ford to the moor. The clan assembled near the bridge, to wave goodbye, and Arteg made a point of smiling at the children, who had stern faces. There was quiet concern, more than fear, and it did not seem fair that the warriors should be leaving Penhal again so soon.

"Let's run up the pathway," offered Cunval. "We can watch them cross the moor and see them cross the valley below."

Running at a steady trot seemed the best thing to do in the circumstances, and when the horses finally disappeared over the last brow of the moor, it was some while before they were sighted again, down in the valley.

"I hope they catch those Saxons and cut their heads off," said Olwen bitterly. The other children agreed and Rees pretended to throw a spear in the general direction.

"I hope they sail back down with the tide and go far away," offered Cunval, but he was not sure whether he really meant it. "Anyway, I'm going to walk back the long way round to the south. It should be possible to see Abermenei from there, on such a clear day. Who's going to run?"

Eventually, the party arrived back at Penhal, but there was not much enthusiasm for play. Cunval busied himself with Henbut and the labourers, in an effort to keep his mind occupied.

After two lonely nights, there was no news. On the third morning, the younger women and the children had gone onto the moor. There was a flush of mushrooms and fungi ready for drying in the houses, and the old couple, Olivia and Anton, had decided to visit Cunval's enclosure, and then go on to the moor to help. As they slowly made their way up the pathway with their sticks, Cunval decided to visit his kiln. Helga, who was now showing her pregnancy, said she would tend Cunval's garden and look after Wolf, rather than be a nuisance to the others.

It was a grey morning, with rain threatening, so Cunval decided to sing a medley of psalms. Ravens, croaking high in the sky, caused him to look up; it was indeed a bleak day. After reaching inside the kiln to clean out the sooty interior, Cunval's face and shaven forehead were covered in black streaks.

There were so many stones lying about from the earlier construction of the kiln that Cunval decided to spread them out and make a platform to stand on. This would make life easier in the winter, when the kiln might be put to further use.

A while later, Cunval stood back and stretched. He started to stamp on the stones, to try to level them up, and, for a moment, he was hardly conscious of the shouts on the moor. He jerked his head up to listen; surely he was dreaming. No, the cry of "Saxons! Saxons!" came clearly from the hill above. In a frenzy, Cunval grabbed his staff and raced up the hill through the wood. The shouts and screams grew louder and louder, and as Cunval burst onto the path near his enclosure, the women and children were running terrified down the pathway towards him.

"Stop them, Cunval. Stop them. They have killed Anton and Olivia."

A fleeing Anhared pushed the children in front of her. Cunval was dumbstruck. Helga had come out onto the path with Wolf, and, when they looked up towards the moor, the pathway was empty. Suddenly, two huge figures crashed through the gorse and bracken above Cunval's garden. They were hung with animal skins and brandishing long heavy swords; Cunval was transfixed with fear at his first sight of fearsome Saxon warriors.

As the two mighty Saxons stamped their way towards Cunval, he instinctively held out his arms.

"Don't hurt the children," he screamed at them. They hesitated at the sight of this strange Celtic shaman, with blackened face, arms outstretched and staff held high. Cunval's tunic billowed in the breeze.

"Don't hurt the children," shouted Helga in the Saxon tongue. "Go away, you murderers!"

As the Saxons stopped in their tracks and Wolf snarled at their heels, Cunval repeated in the Saxon tongue, "Go away, go away."

Helga lunged forward at the nearest Saxon; he instinctively hit her with the butt of his sword and sent her sprawling against the wattle fence. Cunval rushed at the enraged warrior just as his comrade raised his sword arm. Cunval did not even feel the blow that struck him down; he sank to the ground, eyes wide open. His last sight on this Earth was the clouded face of Helga, a few feet away. Dear Cunval was no more.

Brockvael had been dozing when the shouts brought him to his feet. He grabbed his sword and rushed from the hall to the gateway. The women and children were scrambling across the bridge, and the labourers were racing from the barn, armed with pitchforks.

"What's happened?" shouted Brockvael.

"Two Saxons have killed Anton and Olivia. They're coming down the pathway. Stop them, Brockvael," Anhared cried.

She ushered the children into the enclosure as an infuriated Brockvael marched to the river. Cam was the first to leap onto the bridge and make his way across the swinging walkway.

"Wait there, Cam," shouted Brockvael.

He could see two figures striding down the pathway from the moor, and instinct told him that the best place to meet them was on the bridge. The river below was now too high to wade across successfully; these devils must be stopped here and now.

"Steady, Cam. Jab with your fork when they come close," ordered Brockvael.

He was an old campaigner and knew that having Cam in the way would slow the Saxons. Cam was grim-faced and angry; he had become a different person in these circumstances. Brockvael motioned the other labourers to stand ready as the dreaded enemy clambered up the other side of the bridge. The Saxons looked angry; they were not going to be stopped by a bunch of farmers. Cam started thrusting at the first Saxon, when got to the middle of the bridge and tried to slash at Cam's raised pitchfork. Cam was knocked onto the side ropes and, as the Saxon swung downwards with his sword, Cam dived forward and the mighty blow sliced through the side ropes behind him. Just as the second Saxon made a swipe at Cam, an arrow whistled through the air and sunk deeply into his arm. Cam grabbed the howling man's legs as the first Saxon stamped forward to slash at Brockvael. The old champion knew exactly what to do; he moved forward to parry the blow and, in one swift movement, he jabbed forward, his sword-blade slicing across the Saxon's neck. Then, reeling backwards from a kick in the knee, the Saxon was hardly even aware of Brockvael's sword-point piercing his heart. His comrade behind had struck downwards with his sword-butt onto Cam's head, but then a second arrow screeched through the air and pierced straight through his cheekbone into his brain. His raised sword-arm dropped for the last time. Cam, stunned, rolled off the planking into the swirling water below. His comrades waded into the river and pulled him, gasping, onto the bank.

Brockvael, for a moment, stood motionless, his hands gripping the side ropes and his sword standing upright in the enemy chest. He turned to Henbut, who knelt on the bank, his bow-tip resting on the ground.

"I'd almost forgotten your skill with the bow, Henbut.

You did a good job, and so did you, Cam." Cam sat on the riverbank, nursing a bleeding head-wound, his legs still dangling in the water.

One of the labourers had rushed to the palisades, to shout out the news, and slowly the whole community emerged to survey the unbelievable battle scene. The distraught women held their hands over their mouths, in horror at what might have been.

"It was a close thing," muttered Brockvael. "Maponus has saved us."

"Sire," Henbut moved onto the bridge, and asked, "can I go up to Cunval's place?"

"Oh, no," gasped Anhared, "and Helga? Where is she?"

chapter 28

Henbut stepped over the two Saxon bodies and hurried across the bridge. He was fearful for Cunval and Helga, for he knew in his heart that the Saxons would not have spared them. As he ran and clambered up the pathway, he could hear the women close behind. The moment he saw Cunval, face down, he knew that he was not of this world. Henbut's heart plunged into grief.

"This is a tragedy," he cried out, as the women ran up. Helga groaned when the women turned her and wiped her bloody forehead.

"Thank God, she's alive." Anhared cradled her in her arms and gently rocked her.

The children stood weeping a little way down the path, waiting for a signal from the adults. Henbut went to Cunval's hut and returned with his priest's hooded cloak. He spread it over Cunval's head and shoulders, covering the wound that had severed the vertebrae of his thin neck. Brave Wolf lay dead at Cunval's feet, as if asleep.

Henbut then motioned to the children to join the grief-stricken women and to see the carnage. They kept their distance, unable to believe what their eyes were seeing.

"Cunval, Cunval," they sobbed.

Rees moved forward and knelt by Wolf. One of the labourers ran breathlessly up the pathway.

"Brockvael says to come back to the bridge as soon as

you've finished here, Henbut. He's worried that there may be more Saxons about, and he orders that we must all stay at the bridge."

Henbut nodded as the labourer surveyed the scene and weighed up the situation, ready to report to Brockvael.

"You children, go back," ordered Henbut. "Now, ladies, before we get Helga back down, let's put Cunval into his hut."

The women had propped Helga against the fence because she insisted that she was all right. Luckily, her wound had resulted from a glancing blow. They each took a grip on Cunval's tunic and dragged his lifeless body into the hut. Henbut laid him out correctly, and then dragged Wolf into the hut, to lie beside him.

Gwenhaen took charge of conveying Helga to safety, and Anhared joined Henbut for the gruesome task of looking for the bodies of Olivia and Anton. Despite his advanced years, Henbut had tears in his eyes, and a feeling of utter dejection in his heart. Sudden death in this fashion and the awful sight of beloved Cunval's body defied any logical thought.

The moor had never looked as gloomy as it did now, under the cloudy sky, and a fine drizzle had set in. It did not take long to find the bodies of the elderly couple, who had suffered massive sword-blows to the head, and whose death had been swift.

Anhared related the story. "Anton and Olivia came across the Saxons hiding in the heather," she explained. "They gave the alarm and then fended off the Saxons with their sticks. That gave the rest of us chance to run. Cunval came up through the wood, and he must have tried to stop them.

It gave us all time to get across the bridge."

Henbut nodded; he had been trained as a warrior as a young man, but had never had to go to war.

"We must cover them up. I'll use my cloak," said Anhared "Can you pull them closer together?"

They laid the couple close together on a bed of heather; Henbut closed their eyelids and covered their upper bodies with the cloak. He and Anhared were discussing what to do next, when horses appeared in the distance. For a brief moment, Henbut and Anhared stared intently, not knowing whether more Saxons were on the loose. Then, Arteg and the warriors galloped towards them. Arteg was furious when he heard what had happened in his absence. He was so angry with himself at having left the settlement unguarded, and, after examining the bodies in front of him, he stormed off, leading his tired horse by the reins.

The other warriors put the bodies across their horses, and they all walked briskly down the hill. Arteg had stopped at Cunval's hut, to confirm the sad demise of the priest. Cunval had been at Penhal for such a short space of time, yet had somehow softened the rigid routine of warrior life. There would now be a huge gap in the children's lives.

The others caught up, and soon there was a procession down to the bridge. Two of the warriors led the horses downstream, to the fording place, and watched Arteg climb onto the bridge to examine the lifeless Saxons. Brockvael greeted Arteg and a serious discussion ensued, out of earshot of the others. One of the warriors rode on a fresh horse to Abermenei. Through an established relay system, news of the Saxon incursion and the skirmish would be with all the war bands by nightfall.

That evening Brockvael got drunk. He had avenged, in some way, the death of his dear son Catvael, and Gwenhaen seemed to encourage him into oblivion for the night. Helga was recovering in her room, and the women took it in turns to stay with her. The mood in the hall was sombre; in Henbut's house, among the labourers, there was muted discussion of the day's events, despite Cam suffering with a crushing headache. He had been allowed a full mug of wine, and, tomorrow, he would be a hero; he drank to his dead friends, and cried.

Early the next morning, Cynvarch galloped once more into the Penhal enclosure. He had arrived at Abermenei the evening before and been hugely relieved to learn of the killing of the Saxons, despite the tragic Penhal deaths. Warriors had been immediately sent to scour the countryside to the east and to check on all the outlying farms. It appeared that the two young, shipwrecked Saxons had done what none of the commanders had expected. After being shipwrecked in the estuary, they had turned inland, to try to reach the coast further to the south, perhaps finding the opportunity to steal a boat. Once discovered on the moor, they had only one option open to them: to kill the whole community at Penhal, steal some food, and then escape in an unknown direction.

Cynvarch inspected the Saxon bodies, which still lay on show on the bridge, and congratulated Brockvael, whose name would undoubtedly go down in Celtic history. He commiserated with Arteg, saying that he had correctly followed orders and that he, Cynvarch, was the one guilty of not anticipating all the dangers.

Tidiog, at Abermenei, was broken-hearted. Pedur sent

for him on the previous evening, after the message from Penhal arrived. Pedur suggested that Tidiog and some Christian helpers set off for Penhal the next morning. When they arrived at noon, Cynvarch had already departed for Caerleon.

There was to be a funeral at Cunval's cemetery on the third day. Tidiog and his companions were in time to witness the decapitation of the dead Saxons and see their heads grotesquely impaled on two poles overlooking the deep pool. Their bodies had been stripped for trophies, and a funeral pyre was being prepared, ready for the commitment of their ashes to the waiting spirit ancestors of the river.

Tidiog's sad procession up the pathway to the site of Cunval's martyrdom left him with the duty of entering Cunval's now silent hut. He was devastated by the sight of his dead colleague. Prayers were commenced and psalms sung. Tidiog decided to bury Wolf by the side of the pathway, where a stone marker could be placed for all to see for years to come.

Henbut had accompanied the group and explained that Anton and Olivia were admirers of Cunval and had expressed a wish that they should, in due course, be buried in Cunval's cemetery alongside Freid. Brockvael had consented to this, probably with some relief. The congregation now had the rest of the day to dig three graves, all of equal prominence, and all to lie east to west. There was no time to make wooden coffins, so Henbut showed them the scree of rocks close by, with which rough, stone-sided grave cists were prepared, complete with flat capstones.

The arrangement was that Tidiog and his friends would sleep in Henbut's house that night. The labourers had willingly accepted retirement to the barn with some ale. By nightfall, the last remains of the Saxon warriors had been given to the river, and their heads were left facing the deep pool. There had been no ceremony; Durwit's obsolete rituals and chants were gone from the valley for ever. Brockvael, however, had spent some time at his dead shaman's shrine in the grotto of the spring.

During the third day, Tidiog had made arrangements for the funeral procession to start at the Penhal north gateway. He was leaving enough time for any dignitaries from Caerleon to travel by horse. He was certainly expecting his bishop, Dyfrig, and the deacon, Aidan, to come to Penhal. This would be normal practice, and the grief of losing a brother could be shared, but when a long procession suddenly appeared along the west track-way, the whole community was in a panic.

King Myric, with a grim-faced Cynan, led a band of bodyguards and officials, followed by Bishop Dyfrig, his deacon, Aidan, and also Madoc of Caer Bigga.

The king dismounted and warmly shook hands with his old comrade, Brockvael. Cynan embraced Arteg, and introductions were formally made all round. Two benches and a table were set in the field, for the king and Brockvael to hold a private discussion, while the whole clan made preparations for the funeral and the evening banquet.

Tidiog and his group took the bishop to the quiet of the riverbank, avoiding the spectacle of the enemy heads overlooking the pool. Bishop Dyfrig was an imposing figure in his light robe; he was nearly seventy, though his kindly disposition and thin grey hair made him look older. He was not of athletic physique, but his movements were positive and assured. The children were called over to meet him, and he spoke with them easily about Cunval and their lost friendship. He explained that he had received good reports of the kindness of the people of both Penhal and Abermenei, and looked forward to the day when Rees and Conmael would be visiting Caerleon.

Bishop Dyfrig turned to Tidiog. "After I have consecrated the cemetery, you're entirely in charge of the service, Tidiog. The rest of us will sing with you and say prayers after you have given a sermon." The bishop smiled at his nervous priest. "Now, don't worry, my son, Cunval will be with you."

Cynan eventually joined the sad gathering, and addressed Tidiog. "My brother Cunval's parents, his and mine, are too heavy with grief to travel. They will come to you at Abermenei in a few weeks time, Tidiog, and they will be glad for you to show them around. Thank you for everything."

A little later, Bishop Dyfrig led the procession across the bridge and up the hillside. Penhal had never seen such a distinguished procession. Almost everybody was able to stand within the enclosure, but Brockvael and the warriors kept their pagan dignity by remaining in the gateway. The bishop and his clergy blessed the spring and then walked around the boundary of the cemetery, sprinkling holy water, to confirm the Christian consecration of Cunval's legacy. The funeral service was brief and the impassioned sermon from Tidiog struck a chord with all, pagan and Christian alike. The women and children wept. The men held back tears.

The wise bishop smiled softly at the congregation. He knew, deep in his heart, that in the fullness of time, the children of the district, together with Helga's baby, would all benefit from the goodness and bravery of a young priest and an elderly couple. A strong, new generation would emerge. Bishop Dyfrig and Tidiog later stood together at Cunval's small pool, now consecrated and holy.

"Remember, dear Tidiog, our good work must go on. We must be strong and never give in. Next spring, a new young priest will come to Penhal. Until then, look after the children. They are our future."

The bishop's eyes moistened and clouded over. Cunval had sown the seeds, and the tearful brethren of today would complete his work tomorrow.

Other titles from the popular dinas imprint

A journey of humour and tragedy…

WHEN THE KIDS GROW UP
Ken James
A gripping drama based on a true story, spanning three decades, set in Dowlais.
0 86243 716 4
£6.95

... and a magical, scary mystery!

SHAPESHIFTERS AT CILGERRAN
Liz Whittaker
Join in Leo and Ginny's thrilling adventures. Book 2 of the Dreamstealers Trilogy.
0 86243 719 9
£5.95

dinas

Titles already published

Shapeshifters at Cilgerran – Liz Whittaker £5.95
Germs – Dai Vaughan £5.95
Cunval's Mission – David Hancocks £5.95
When the Kids Grow Up – Ken James £6.95
The Church Warden – Lillian Comer £7.95
The Fizzing Stone – Liz Whittaker £4.95
A Dragon To Agincourt – Malcom Pryce £7.95
Aberdyfi: Past and Present – Hugh M Lewis £6.95
Aberdyfi: The Past Recalled – Hugh M Lewis £6.95
Ar Bwys y Ffald – Gwilym Jenkins £7.95
Black Mountains – David Barnes £6.95
Choose Life! – Phyllis Oostermeijer £5.95
Clare's Dream – J Gillman Gwynne £4.95
Cwpan y Byd a dramâu eraill – J O Evans £4.95
Dragonrise – David Morgan Williams £4.95
Dysgl Bren a Dysgl Arian – R Elwyn Hughes £9.95
In Garni's Wake – John Rees £7.95
Stand Up and Sing – Beatrice Smith £4.95
The Dragon Wakes – Jim Wingate £6.95
The Wonders of Dan yr Ogof – Sarah Symons £6.95
You Don't Speak Welsh – Sandi Thomas £5.95

*For more information about this innovative imprint,
contact Lefi Gruffudd at lefi@ylolfa.com
or go to www.ylolfa.com/dinas.
A Dinas catalogue is also available.*